# Love
# Hurts

D0835199

LOOK FOR THE OTHER BOOKS IN THIS
INSPIRATIONAL SERIES FROM BANTAM BOOKS.

COMING IN SUMMER 2000:

*The Diaries*
a Clearwater Crossing Special Edition

# clearwater crossing

# Love
# Hurts

## laura peyton roberts

BANTAM BOOKS
NEW YORK • TORONTO • LONDON • SYDNEY • AUCKLAND

RL 5.8, age 12 and up
LOVE HURTS
A Bantam Book / April 2000

ISBN: 0-553-49299-3

Visit us on the Web! www.randomhouse.com/teens
Educators and librarians, for a variety of teaching tools, visit us at
www.randomhouse.com/teachers

Published simultaneously in the United States and Canada

Bantam Books is an imprint of Random House Children's Books, a
division of Random House, Inc. BANTAM BOOKS and the rooster
colophon are registered trademarks of Random House, Inc. Bantam
Books, 1540 Broadway, New York, New York, 10036.

PRINTED IN THE UNITED STATES OF AMERICA

OPM   10   9   8   7   6   5   4   3   2   1

*For my readers,*
*with thanks*

*We love because he first loved us.*

*1 John 4:19*

# One

"I said, what are you doing in that safe?" Mr. Andrews repeated angrily. He swayed slightly in the Andrewses' library doorway but seemed to be growing more sober by the second. "What are those papers you're looking at? Answer me!"

Terrified, Melanie tore her eyes away from her father and snatched up the birth certificates she'd just dropped. More family papers lay strewn about the floor where she sat, and the heart-shaped garnet necklace Trent Wheeler had given her mother was lying out in plain sight. "I was just—just—"

"Just snooping where you don't belong!" he said, striding toward her in a surprisingly direct line.

He had sounded out of it when he'd first burst into the room, but now his voice had sharpened. His eyes held hers in a harsh, steady gaze, and his steps barely wavered as he walked. He was an experienced alcoholic, and Melanie had seen him suppress the effects of drinking many times before—she'd just never seen him do it so fast.

*He must really be furious*, she thought, imagining anger burning the liquor out of his system as if he were some sort of human flambé. *I'm such an idiot to have tried this with him in the house!*

Reaching her, he bent to snatch the birth certificates from her fingers. She watched, paralyzed, as his hand stretched toward the truth she had worked so hard to find, ready to rip it away. . . .

"No!" she cried, yanking the papers out of his grasp. She scrambled to her feet, backing as she rose. Despite her fear, she kept the yellowed old documents clutched to her chest, the names at their tops already burned into her brain. "Who's Angel Wheeler?"

Mr. Andrews froze. He stared at her a moment, as if not sure what he'd heard, and then he seemed to deflate like an old beach ball. His shoulders stooped; the angry color drained from his face. He rubbed a hand across his stubbly chin, then covered his bloodshot eyes. "This isn't how we wanted to tell you."

"Tell me what, Dad? That I have a sister somewhere?"

The instant she spoke, Melanie realized she had to be right. She sucked in a deep breath, eyes popping with her discovery. If Angel was her mother's daughter with Trent . . .

But her father shook his head, his gaze on the floor. "It's not like that, Melanie. Not exactly, anyway."

Feeling slightly bolder, she double-checked the paper on top of her stack. *Name: Angel Allen Wheeler. Mother: Tristyn Allen Wheeler.*

"No? It sure looks that way to me. Where is she, Dad?"

He took a step toward her, but Melanie drew back until her spine was against a bookcase.

"You don't understand," he insisted.

"Then why don't you explain it?"

His mouth opened and closed a few times. He shook his head as if trying to clear it. "Why don't we . . . ? Downstairs. I need coffee."

He turned and left the room as abruptly as he'd come in, leaving her pressed against the wall. The door to the safe still stood wide open; the mess she had made still littered the floor. It was as if the scene between them had never happened.

Then the sound of her father's slippers slapping the marble staircase jolted her back to the present . . . and all the questions that were still unanswered. Hesitating just long enough to slip the garnet necklace into her pocket, Melanie followed her father.

By the time she reached the kitchen, he was already at the sink, filling a mug of instant coffee with hot water from the tap. She started to take a seat at the breakfast bar, but he motioned her over to the nearby sitting room. They sat down on the cold

3

leather furniture, the backyard beyond the windows black with night. Mr. Andrews fiddled with his coffee, swirling the liquid around the cup. When he finally looked up, he seemed to have come to some sort of decision.

"The first thing you ought to know is that your mother always intended to tell you what I'm about to," he said. "She never meant to keep it a secret. She was just waiting for you to be old enough to understand . . . and then . . . then . . ."

*Then she died,* Melanie filled in silently.

"Melanie, your mother had been married once before she met me. She was young, and impulsive, and the entire thing was a disaster. She wanted you to know, because she hoped you'd learn from her mistakes." Her father sighed. "And because of Angel."

"Tris married a guy she met in high school. She blew off college at the last minute and followed him down here from Iowa. His name was Trent Wheeler, and he said he wanted to marry her right away, but he was a liar, as it turned out. They were here six months before they finally got married. Living in sin, your grandparents called it—they were so angry they didn't even come to the wedding. Eight months later, Angel was born.

"By then your mom already knew she had made some bad choices, but she loved that little girl. Trent was staying out all night, and your grandparents ac-

4

cused her of marrying him because she was pregnant, but Tristyn said that as miserable as they all made her, Angel made her twice that happy." He drained the last of the lukewarm coffee and put down his cup.

"What happened?" Melanie prompted breathlessly.

"Crib death. SIDS. Angel was only a couple of months old."

Melanie gasped, stunned. She felt the loss of what could have been, but not grief, not exactly. Angel's life was still too unreal for her death to cause that type of pain. A little sadness, disappointment . . .

Mostly, she felt for her mother.

"Poor Mom," she said at last, remembering the naïve teenage Tristyn whose diary she had read.

Her father nodded. "She was devastated. Trent wasn't there for her, and her own parents tried to make it her fault. None of it would have happened, they said, if she'd been married in church and lived in a proper house instead of some filthy apartment."

Mr. Andrews's voice had become angry. "They treated her like dirt. I think they really believed they'd have the upper hand all her life, like they'd never forgive her and she'd always be crawling. But in the end, she was the one who couldn't forgive. When they didn't want to come to *our* wedding, she cut them right out of her life."

"Why didn't they want—?"

"They never liked me, Melanie. They never

*approved* of me. Maybe they knew what I thought of them. I don't know."

He rubbed his temples and slouched back in his seat. "Your mom and Trent split up after Angel died. He went home, so she stayed here, working. The next year she enrolled in CU. I met her there one day when my Intro to Surveying class was making a map of the campus."

His eyes grew distant. "She was painting a landscape, and I was walking backward over the lawn with one of those stupid stadia rods. Bill Parker was trying to line me up in his sights and he kept waving me over and back, over and back. Finally, I stepped back right over Tristyn's easel. I think that was actually Bill's plan all along. The whole thing came crashing down, paint everywhere . . ." The smile on her father's face was exquisitely sad. "I loved her instantly."

He rose abruptly. "That's enough for one night. If there's anything else you want to know, you can ask me tomorrow."

"One last thing," Melanie said quickly. "Where is Angel buried?"

"Next to your mother." He shook his head sadly. "I'm so sorry, Melanie, about . . . all of it. Just know that your mom loved you. Because you can only imagine how much."

He shuffled off, leaving her staring at the blackness outside. Everything fit now. All the unhappiness made sense.

And yet there had been joy, too. Melanie knew her mother had been happy in Clearwater Crossing—incredibly happy, in fact. She had loved Melanie's father, and Melanie, and their big concrete house. Maybe, in a way, her painful past had made her later contentment that much greater.

*So maybe there's still hope for me.*

Rising from the sofa, she pressed a hand to the window, as if an answering hand might press back from the other side. Her flesh met only her own reflection. Would she ever find a guy who'd make the bad things fade away? Someone who would love her as completely as her father had loved her mother?

Melanie laid her cheek on the cool glass. Was there anyone like that out there for her?

"I'm sure he'll be all right," Leah Rosenthal said, not sure of any such thing.

Hunched over in an intensive care waiting room chair, Miguel del Rios spoke without lifting his face from his hands. "This shouldn't be happening."

"I know."

Ever since Miguel's favorite kid at the hospital, nine-year-old Wilms' tumor patient Zachary Dewey, had gone into cardiac arrest earlier that Friday night, Miguel had barely said anything else. He had called her in hysterics, raving about Code Blues and intubation and lots of other things Leah didn't understand. By the time she'd arrived at the hospital, though, Zach was in intensive care and Miguel had shut down almost completely. For the last hour he'd barely let her see his face, but Leah knew his cheeks were wet. Hers were wet too as she put an arm around his shoulders, trying to comfort him.

*When are they going to tell us something?* she wondered, knowing the only thing that would truly help Miguel was hearing that Zach had pulled through.

A few chairs away, on the other side of the waiting room, Mrs. Dewey sat by herself, her face turned toward the wall. She had said hello when Leah had first come in, but since then she'd been silent, wringing a handkerchief in her nervous hands. Leah could see them in her lap now, still at last. The woman's head was bowed, and Leah had the strong impression she was praying.

*It must be awful to have your kid have cancer,* Leah thought, overcome with sympathy. It was even worse for Mrs. Dewey—her husband was dead and Zach was her only child. *To know that he could die, and there's not a thing you can do about it . . .*

Miguel had told her that the type of kidney cancer Zachary had was normally easy to cure, but in Zach's case the tumor was so large that it extended up the vena cava into his heart, complicating surgery. There were cancerous spots on the boy's lungs as well, but even so, his doctors had remained optimistic.

*I wonder how optimistic they are now.* It was horrible to contemplate, but Zach's life could already be over.

At last the ICU door opened. A doctor walked out and headed straight for Mrs. Dewey. Leah could tell just by the man's face that Zach was still alive.

"Look! Look, Miguel," she urged in a whisper. "Is that Dr. Wells?"

Miguel shook his head, his eyes now glued to the doctor.

"He's okay. He's stable now," Leah heard the man tell Mrs. Dewey. "We're still trying to work out exactly what happened, but it was either a toxicity reaction to the chemo drugs or some movement of the tumor thrombus in his atrium."

"Can I see him?" Mrs. Dewey asked shakily.

"Sure. He's unconscious, and he's on a ventilator, but you can come in for a minute." The doctor took her elbow and led her back through the door into the ICU.

"There! Did you hear that? He's okay," Leah said the moment Mrs. Dewey and the doctor had disappeared.

But Miguel looked far from reassured. "They're supposed to be shrinking the tumor so they can cut it out, not poisoning him. He could have died." Miguel's voice was shaking. His hands shook too as he pushed them back through his dark hair. "This was not the plan."

Leah could feel how scared he still was as she put her arms around him.

"You know these are good doctors, and you know they care about Zach," she said softly, her lips against his ear. "I thought you trusted them, Miguel."

He took a few deep breaths. "I do. It's just . . . this wasn't supposed to happen."

Leah kept her arms around him until gradually he relaxed against her body. His breathing slowed. His eyes dropped closed.

*Is he praying too?* she wondered. Even though his eyes were closed, his expression seemed intense. Shutting her eyes on impulse, Leah added a prayer of her own.

*God, I know I don't talk to you much. I'm not even sure if you're there. But I want you to be. I really do. Please . . . watch out for this little boy. He's so young, and probably scared, and his mother obviously loves him a lot.*

Opening her eyes, Leah snuck a sideways peek at Miguel.

*I get the feeling she's not the only one.*

"That's it! Get the dictionary!" Jesse Jones exploded. "I don't care how good you think it sounds, 'jippy' is not a word."

"Uh-huh!" his twelve-year-old stepsister, Brittany, insisted. Instead of leaving the dining room table to get the dictionary, she leaned closer to make her point, the overhead light shining on her blond hair as she pointed to the Scrabble board. "Like if something is a rip-off, it's a jip. It's *jippy*."

"That's *g-y-p*, idiot. If you're going to cheat, I'm not going to play anymore."

Exasperated, he glanced at his watch. "This was already boring, and now it's getting late."

"I'm *not* an idiot, Jesse, and I wasn't cheating, either!" Brittany's brown eyes were wide with indignation. Her chin actually quivered a little. "You'd better take that back."

"Fine, I take it back. Geez, I'm sorry, all right?" Ever since she had run away a few months earlier, he'd been trying harder to get along with her—but did she have to be so sensitive? "Look. I'm tired, and you're obviously tired. Why don't we call it a tie? You ought to be in bed anyway."

Their parents had gone to bed at least an hour before. The house was dark except for the dining room light.

Reluctantly, Brittany began putting letter tiles from the board back into the box. "What about you? Aren't you going to bed?"

"Yeah. Pretty soon."

But when the game was finally put away, when

11

Brittany cast him one last pouty look before heading upstairs, Jesse made no move to follow. Instead he waited until he heard her door click shut; then he slipped out into the garage and climbed into his BMW.

The garage door opened on a sky full of stars. Jesse rolled his car back into the street, hoping his parents wouldn't wake up. He wasn't going to be gone long. Not very long, anyway. But there was something gnawing inside him, something pulling him out that night. He'd never be able to sleep until the ritual had been completed, his pointless curiosity satisfied.

At last the Andrewses' mansion came into view, dark against a barely lighter sky, like a black hole in the stars. His headlights swept halfway up the concrete walls before he switched them off, quickly killing his engine as well. From the interior of his car, he could just make out the windows of Melanie's room, upstairs in the front.

*What is she doing?* he wondered. Was she asleep? Or was she lying awake in the dark, longing for him the way he longed for her?

"Good one!" he snorted. "Keep dreaming, Jones."

As messed up as things were between him and Melanie, he didn't even know why he was there. In fact, there was only one thing he knew for sure: He wished he hadn't been quite so adamant about swearing never to take her back. He had vowed when she broke up with him in January that he would make her suffer. He'd even predicted she'd change her mind and want him back. He'd said then that she could beg all she wanted and it wouldn't change a thing.

The problem was, he hadn't actually expected that to happen, and when Melanie had started kissing up to him not even a week later, he hadn't known what to think. Was she sorry? Or was all the sudden attention just more of the jerking around he had learned to expect from her? He had still been so angry then that it had been easy to tell himself he wanted nothing to do with Melanie Andrews.

But he did. It was all he wanted, in fact. And now, two months later, pretending otherwise was getting a whole lot harder.

*Besides, what if she really is sorry? What if she does want me back?*

If he kept on ignoring her, how much longer would she care? It wasn't as if there weren't a hundred guys at school just dying to snatch her up. Could it be *that* hard to swallow his pride?

*Yes. Because what if I'm wrong and she doesn't want me back? No way am I going to be Melanie's fool again!*

He'd lost track of how many times he'd been down that road already.

*If she'd just say something first . . . If she'd give me some clear sign . . .*

Sighing, Jesse started his engine and turned for

home. At least they were speaking to each other now. At least they had more or less agreed to be friends.

*Friends. That's about as much comfort as an aspirin during a heart attack. It might help in the long run, but not when you're lying there gripping your chest.*

Still . . . what more could he do?

*Maybe me and Melanie just aren't meant to be.*

# Two

"So! A whole week off!" Jenna Conrad's older sister Caitlin teased. "What are you going to do with yourself?"

"I don't know," Jenna admitted, forcing herself to sit up in bed. It was still pretty early, but normally she'd have been up long before, especially on the first day of vacation. "Spring break just doesn't seem that exciting this year."

Caitlin chuckled as she peeled off her wet socks. She had a full-time job working for a veterinarian, but she also ran a dog-walking business on evenings and weekends. She had just returned from her Saturday-morning walking appointments, and her cheeks were still flushed from the cold.

"Any vacation sounds good to me. Between Dr. Campbell, my dogs, and the time we've been spending at the hospital with Sarah, I've barely been able to breathe. It's a good thing Abby goes to work with me, or I'd never see her at all," Caitlin added, smiling at the shaggy gray mutt curled up in a corner of their room.

"You're right. A vacation will be great," Jenna said, trying to sound as if she meant it. At least she wouldn't be selfish enough to complain about it again. She pulled her robe on over her flannel pajamas, lifted a hairbrush off the nightstand, and listlessly began brushing her long brown hair.

"Do you and Peter have lots of plans?" Caitlin asked, inadvertently hitting on the real source of Jenna's unhappiness.

"Uh, not lots. I'm going to the hospital today, and probably tomorrow and Monday. But if Sarah really gets out on Tuesday like she's supposed to, I'll have plenty of time to see Peter later in the week."

"David's coming home next weekend," Caitlin revealed shyly, a blush creeping into her cheeks. "His school has the week *after* Easter off."

"Oh, same as Mary Beth's." Jenna was about to press for more details when the doorbell rang, startling them both.

"Jenna!" Allison called from downstairs. "Peter's here!"

"What?" said Jenna, looking down at her pajamas. What was he doing at her house so early? Especially when she wasn't expecting him? "He could have called first!"

She considered trying to get dressed in a hurry, then changed her mind. It was better if he saw her in her pajamas, actually, so he'd know he was there too early.

"Coming!" she shouted, pushing her feet into fuzzy pink slippers.

"Aren't you going to change?" Caitlin asked, a hint of horror in her voice.

"Nope. If he wants to drop in on people at the crack of dawn, he has to face the consequences."

"It's nine-thirty," Caitlin protested as Jenna walked out their door.

Allison was standing at the base of the ground-floor staircase. Her eyes popped when she caught sight of Jenna.

"Where is he?" Jenna asked impatiently, ignoring her sister's expression.

"In the den." Allison pointed. "But if I were you, I'd change."

"If I were you, I'd mind my own business," Jenna retorted, striding past her.

Peter was standing alone at the den windows, his back to the doorway. Pale spring sunlight flooded through the glass, washing his dark blond hair until the stray strands looked almost platinum. She could just see the edge of his profile, the strong line of his jaw. She anticipated his turning toward her and smiling, a flash of perfect white teeth, and her heart nearly skipped a beat. For a moment she wished she *had* changed. . . .

And then Peter wheeled around.

"What is the *matter* with you?" he demanded. "I asked you about a hundred times if you were upset

17

with me about something, and you said no every time."

Jenna stopped breathing. How had he found out?

"I—uh—"

"Oh, no. You can't tell *me*," he continued sarcastically, "the one person who ought to know, but you don't mind blabbing to Leah. Tell me something, Jenna: How is Leah supposed to undo the fact that Melanie and I kissed?"

"We—We were just talking," Jenna defended herself. "Friends do that."

"I thought you and I were friends!"

Peter's blue eyes were snapping; his chest heaved angrily. Jenna found herself backing up even though there was plenty of room between them.

"I just . . . it seemed like you had to know," she said. "I mean, it was obvious to—"

"Then why did you say you forgave me? You were *lying* to me, Jenna!"

"No. You're making a big deal about noth—"

"It *is* a big deal! I haven't slept all night just thinking about what a big deal it is. If I can't trust you, Jenna, if I can't believe what you say—"

"You're the one who kissed Melanie!"

"Melanie kissed me! And what does it matter, anyway? It's not like you and I were together at the time. In fact, if you hadn't been so busy scheming to get Miguel away from Leah—"

"I was not!" she shrieked, horrified. "Is that what you told Leah?"

"Maybe I should have. Is that who we're confiding in now instead of each other?"

"No! I just thought she'd understand how I felt."

"Well, I hope she did, because I sure don't. All I understand is that you've been lying to me, and playing with my emotions, and taking me for granted—and I'm through with it. I'm done apologizing, too. If anything, you ought to apologize to me."

"What are you saying?" she asked, feeling sick. "Are you saying we—"

"I'm saying to let me know when you're over it. And make sure you *are* over it this time, because I'm too old for this junior-high garbage."

He stalked out of the den and through her front doorway before she could form a reply, leaving her stunned. She didn't know whether to run after him or bolt back up to her room and slam the door. Instead she collapsed to the floor, crying bitterly.

Peter had never spoken to her that way before, but that wasn't even the worst thing. The worst thing was the sneaking suspicion that she'd deserved it. Had she been on shaky ground all along? Should she have been more clear about how insecure his kiss with Melanie had made her?

*Even if I had, it wouldn't have changed how I felt.*

Jenna hugged her ribs and rocked back and forth,

feeling as if her heart would break. Peter hadn't been gone five minutes and she already ached to make up. Having him angry with her was ten times worse than being angry with him. But how could she say she was over something that only got worse every day? She'd never intended to lie to him, but she realized now that she had. Should she lie to him again?

*Maybe I'm just not ready to have a boyfriend*, she thought miserably. *Ever since Peter and I got together, things have been so confusing. I liked it better when we were just friends. At least we were friends then.*

She pulled her knees up to her chest, bracing against the pain. *Maybe we should break up.*

It wasn't the first time the idea had crossed her mind, but it was still awful enough to choke her in midsob. She didn't want to end their romance. But losing Peter's friendship would be worse. She'd do anything, anything in the world, to keep that from happening.

Even break up with him.

Nicole Brewster picked up the phone to call Melanie, then set it back down again.

"Make sure you have everything first," she instructed herself, looking over the items before her. She had made her bed for a change that Saturday morning, and arrayed on the smooth bedspread were all the things she needed to practice for cheerleading tryouts. "If Melanie can take the time to coach me on her vacation, the least I can do is be prepared."

Except that she was more than prepared. Anyone could see that. She had practice outfits coordinated in advance for every day of the week, plus two pairs of brand-new pom-poms, just in case one got ruined. Fanned out in sequential order were six back issues of *Cheer!* that she'd scored at the school library, and next to those were two cassette tapes with identical copies of the dance music the cheerleading coach, Sandra Kincaid, had selected for tryouts. On the floor nearby were her boom box and an older pair of running shoes—she was saving her new ones for tryouts. "That's got to be everything. Right?"

"Right." She picked up the phone again, but before she could dial it rang in her hand.

"Hello? Melanie?" Nicole said hopefully.

"Sorry," said Guy Vaughn, her on-again, mostly off-again boyfriend. "I'm not nearly that cute."

"You're right, you're not," Nicole said spitefully, still angry with him about their last embarrassing date at the bowling alley. After she had finally decided that *someone* needed to move things along and had taken a chance by kissing him, not only hadn't he appreciated her initiative, he had told her he didn't think he was ready to take their relationship to that level.

21

*Whatever that means.* She had never been more humiliated. Not by him, anyway.

"So what are you doing today?" he asked. "Anything special?"

"No." She hadn't told him before that she was trying out for cheerleader, and she was too mad at him now to tell him the time.

"Maybe we can get together, then. I was thinking—"

"I mean—oops! I should have said I was busy. Not that it's anything *special.* But I think I'm going to be pretty tied up this week."

"Doing what?"

*Think. Think, Nicole!* she told herself, frantically racking her brain for a weeklong excuse. "Well, it's kind of a charity thing. You know that group I'm in—Eight Prime? We're fixing up a site at the lake for some kids to use as a day camp this summer. Next Saturday we're inviting the whole town out to help, but I have a ton of things to do before then." The fact that they were all totally unrelated to the Junior Explorers was really none of his business.

"Maybe I'll come out."

"Huh? Out where?"

"To the lake. Isn't that what you just said?"

"Oh. Right. But not until Saturday."

"What time? Maybe Jeff and Hope will want to come too."

*No way!* Nicole screamed silently. *If Jeff brings Hope, and Courtney shows up . . .*

She opened her mouth to protest, then reluctantly swallowed her groan. If she made a big deal about Hope's coming, she might have to explain why—and that was the last thing she wanted to do. Besides, Courtney wasn't likely to show up to anything that involved working for free. She had helped at the haunted house, but only because Jeff had practically forced her into it. Now that she was so wrapped up with that sleaze Kyle Snowden, she wasn't apt to volunteer for forestry service.

"Get there whenever you want," said Nicole. "We're going to be working all day."

"Okay. Are you sure you and I can't do something before then?"

He sounded so hopeful that for a moment, Nicole almost wavered. Maybe Guy was coming around. Then she glanced down at the cheerleading stuff on her bed. All she *really* wanted to do was practice, to give herself the best possible chance of making the squad that she could. Why should she have to worry about Guy, and Courtney, and Courtney's stupid ex and his new girlfriend, when she had much bigger fish to fry?

"I'm really pretty tied up. I'm afraid I'll just have to see you Saturday."

If Guy was sorry now for the way he'd treated her,

he was about a week too late. So what if he was a great singer and had his own band? So what if everyone but Courtney seemed to like him? So what if he was even kind of cute? After the way he'd embarrassed her last time, Nicole was pretty sure she never wanted to see Guy Vaughn again.

Miguel leaned back in his pew at All Souls, trying to make sense of the Palm Sunday story he'd just heard. He imagined a man on a donkey riding into Jerusalem and mobs of happy people waving palm fronds in celebration of his arrival. Miguel had always thought that a particularly triumphant entrance, which made it even harder to understand why only a few days later that man had been crucified. How could things have changed so completely so quickly? Shouldn't there have been more warning?

"Miguel. Are you coming?" his sister, Rosa, asked. She was standing with their mother, ready to exit the church. The aisle was already full of people.

"In a minute. I'll meet you out there."

Miguel wanted to be the last to leave that day, to say a final prayer for Zach's recovery. The boy was still in the ICU, but on Saturday Miguel had finally had the chance to talk with Dr. Wells about Zach's condition.

"Zach is fine. I expect he'll be back on the children's ward Monday," the doctor had reported cheerfully. "Better, the chemo is finally getting results and the tumor is retreating. If this keeps up, I'll be operat-

24

ing soon. It'll be a load off everyone's mind to get that surgery behind us."

*To say the least*, Miguel thought now. Like all kids with Wilms' tumor, Zach would have to have his cancerous kidney removed. After Mrs. del Rios's experiences with kidney disease and her recent transplant, Miguel knew that a person could get by quite well with one kidney. He wasn't worried about that. But in Zach's case, with such a large tumor so close to his heart, the surgery itself would be dangerous.

*I don't mean to complain, Lord*, Miguel prayed silently. *You brought Zach this far, and Dr. Wells is a good surgeon. It's just . . . I wish we could get that part over with. I know you have a plan, but could the surgery be soon?*

He prayed awhile longer in that vein, and when he finally opened his eyes, the church was empty. Miguel lingered another moment, feeling he'd connected somehow, then slowly rose to his feet, his senses suddenly heightened. With one last deep breath to hold him, he reached the door and stepped reluctantly into the morning sunshine.

"Miguel!" a female voice cried.

All the calm he had felt a moment before deserted him in a single heartbeat. The voice was Sabrina Ambrosi's.

"What are you doing?" he asked as she ran up. She was dressed as if for a party, black liner surrounding her violet eyes. "I didn't see you inside."

"No, I couldn't make mass. But I wanted to try to catch you." The smile she flashed him was wide and perfect.

"What for?" he asked warily. Ever since Sabrina had made that unexpected move on him, he could barely breathe around her. And now she was making a habit of pouncing on him after mass. . . .

"I saw Eight Prime's ad in this morning's paper. About the work party on Saturday?"

"Oh. Right." With everything going on with Zach, Miguel had forgotten all about the Junior Explorers.

"I'll definitely be there, and I can bring all kinds of stuff my dad has left over from job sites. We can probably build those kids a castle if you want to."

Miguel tried to smile, but inside he was freaking out. A contractor's daughter, Sabrina not only had access to building supplies, she knew what to do with them. She wasn't blowing smoke about that. On the other hand, Leah was going to be there too, and if Sabrina tried anything in front of her . . .

"That's nice of you, but I'm not even sure I'll be going myself. Something's come up at the hospital, and I might have to go there instead."

"Nothing bad, I hope," she said, widening her amazing eyes.

"It's just . . . work. You know how it goes." He really didn't feel like telling her about Zach.

"Well, try to get off," she said. "I don't want to be the only one out there who knows how to pound a nail." She smiled again before she walked off, making his heart sink into his gut.

A whole day in the woods with Sabrina and Leah? *Great. That's all I need.*

# *Three*

"I feel kind of ridiculous practicing here," Melanie told Nicole, glancing around uneasily as she wiped her face with a towel. "People are going to think we're freaks."

"No one's even looking," Nicole said firmly, bending to rewind the cassette in her boom box. "And if they are, they probably just think we're really dedicated."

*Really dedicated freaks*, Melanie thought self-consciously.

True, there was no one else behind the Clearwater Crossing Park activities center that Monday morning, and the few people who could catch glimpses of them from the basketball courts or the playground hadn't shown much interest. Still, Melanie wished they had picked a better place to practice. Her own house was out—she didn't want to risk an encounter between Nicole and her father, who had stayed resolutely drunk since Friday night's big discussion—but there had to be somewhere else.

Nicole straightened up, a pom-pom in each hand. "Ready to do it again?"

They had already done the entire dance four times that day. Not to mention the eight or nine times they'd done it on Sunday—step by step by step. Melanie heard the music in her dreams.

"Not really. Hey, Nicole, why couldn't we practice at your house again?"

"I *told* you. My little sister's a monster. She was spying on us the whole time yesterday. And after you left . . ." Nicole scrunched up her face. "I'm not in the mood for more of her comments, that's all."

"We're just wasting our time now anyway. You've already got this dance down, Nicole. You don't need me anymore."

Nicole's blue eyes held a trace of panic. "No, I do! I have to be perfect! You know how good some of those other girls are, and there are only four spots available."

To come up with that figure, Nicole had to be assuming that the four younger cheerleaders would re-earn their places on the squad of eight. Melanie sighed, knowing she was probably right.

"True, but you're doing really well, Nicole. You ought to start thinking about your original dance instead."

"Really?" Nicole asked breathlessly.

Only the girls who made the first cut would get a

chance to audition an original dance. Melanie belatedly realized she had essentially just admitted she expected Nicole to make the cut. It would be cruel to give the girl false hope. . . .

*But I really do think she'll make it.* The improvement she'd seen in Nicole since the first couple of practices was truly astonishing.

"Have you picked any music yet?" Melanie asked. "The music is really important."

"Well, no. But I've been thinking about some songs." Nicole proceeded to reel off everything currently playing on MTV.

"Just because a song's good to listen to doesn't mean it's good for cheerleading," Melanie ventured cautiously, waiting to see if Nicole would be offended. On the contrary, the girl was hanging on her every word. "It has to have the right kind of beat, and sometimes it's better if it's not too well known. When people hear a song they like, it raises their expectations."

Nicole nodded slowly. "*You* have to pick something for me. Can we go to the mall tomorrow?"

Melanie hesitated at the thought of spending three days in a row with Nicole.

"Please?" Nicole wheedled. "I'll drive, and I'll buy you a CD too."

"All right. But if we're doing that tomorrow, then let's call it quits for today. I have some other things I want to take care of."

Nicole twisted a strand of blond hair that had escaped her ponytail. "Do you want me to drive you home?" she offered. "We could probably put your bike in the trunk."

"That's okay. It's pretty nice out, for a change."

At last Nicole was loaded up and ready to be on her way. "Don't forget tomorrow," she called through the open car window. "I'll call you tonight to make sure."

Melanie waved and swung one leg over her bicycle, eager to be off. It wasn't that hanging out with Nicole was so awful. If anything, they'd been getting along pretty well lately. It was just that she had so many other things on her mind. . . .

She coasted down the hill to the main road, thinking about her mother and Angel. It was bizarre to know that she had once been standing next to Angel's grave, maybe even on it, and had never felt a twinge. Even if she had happened to read the name—Angel Wheeler—she wouldn't have looked twice. The words had meant nothing to her then.

*I should call Aunt Gwen and tell her I know the whole story now*, Melanie thought, still coasting. *For that matter, I should tell my dad I know Aunt Gwen, and that I've already been to Iowa to see Mom's grave.*

But none of those revelations seemed too pressing. The adults had certainly taken their time filling her in on things—now it was their turn to wait. Eventually she'd feel like talking again, but for now she just wanted to think. To turn the pieces over in her mind and see how well they fit . . .

At the corner, Melanie started to turn right, toward her house, then abruptly applied the hand brakes. The old pads squealed against metal rims, and she barely got a foot on the pavement before she slipped off the seat toward the handlebars. A couple of quick hops and she had regained control, turning the bike completely around.

*I'll just make a loop past Jesse's house.*

Sure, it was a little farther—all right, a lot farther—but . . .

*Maybe he'll see me and come outside. I can always say I was just out riding, that passing his house was strictly coincidental. . . .*

She started pedaling in the new direction. Then she turned another U, toward home.

*That's just a bad idea. He would know I was lying, for one thing. And he obviously doesn't like me anymore, so what's the point?*

She still couldn't understand how someone's feelings could change so quickly. Maybe he had never really liked her that much in the first place. But it was time to accept that breaking up with Jesse was a mistake that she'd never be able to fix.

Her legs began moving faster as she pedaled resolutely for home.

*In any event, it's time to stop being so pathetic and start getting on with my life. I don't have to pine for Jesse every minute anymore—or if I do, at least I don't have to let it show. Maybe I ought to go out with someone new, just to get my feet wet.*

A red car passed her on the road, jolting her heart into hyperspeed before she realized it wasn't Jesse's. It wasn't even a nice car. Her pulse kept pounding in the wake of her realization, unable to slow down.

*All right. I should definitely go out with someone else. The prom is coming up in a few weeks. That could be the perfect occasion for resuming life without Jesse.*

She squinted after the disappearing car, and suddenly she realized that some sad, desperate part of her was still trying to turn it into a BMW.

*I'll do it,* she decided, forcing her gaze to her handlebars. *If I put my mind to it, I can have a date for the prom in no time.*

*Maybe she doesn't even know,* Leah thought, hesitating with her finger on Jenna's doorbell. *Maybe Peter didn't tell her.*

It seemed like a lot to hope for.

*Besides, even if he didn't, I should.*

She had been so busy with Miguel most of the weekend that she'd managed not to think too much about the foolish way she'd told Peter that Jenna was still upset with him for kissing Melanie. But now that Zach was out of danger, Leah's crime against her friend was preying on her mind. Jenna had sworn her

33

to secrecy, after all, and she should have respected that. It was just that at the time Leah had been so sure she knew better, that telling Peter the truth might even save her friends' relationship.

She just hadn't expected him to take the news so badly.

*I have to apologize,* Leah decided, pressing the bell. *I probably ought to do it on my knees.*

Jenna answered the door herself, and the moment Leah saw her, she knew she had heard the bad news. Jenna's swollen eyes met hers, then glanced away as if stung. Her long hair needed brushing, and her outfit looked like something that had come from under the bed.

"Jenna, I'm sorry," Leah blurted out before her friend could speak. "You trusted me, and I let you down. I was only trying to help."

Jenna's eyes focused on something to the side of Leah's head.

"But that's no excuse!" Leah added quickly. "I should have kept my big mouth shut."

Still no response from Jenna.

"Can . . . can I come in?"

Jenna shrugged, then turned and walked back into the house, leaving the door wide open. Leah hesitated just long enough to close it behind her before she followed Jenna to the Conrads' den, gabbing nervously all the way.

"I'm sorry I waited this long to come over. I kind

of hoped I'd run into you at the hospital over the weekend, but of course the ICU's on a different floor, and Miguel really needed me. I would have—"

Jenna turned abruptly. "What happened?" she asked, with real fear in her eyes. "What's wrong with Miguel?"

"Didn't you hear? Zach's heart stopped Friday night and he had to be resuscitated. It was really, really scary."

Jenna gasped and put a hand to her throat. "Oh, no! Is he all right?"

"Yes. He's still in the ICU, but his doctors say he's fine, so Miguel's finally calming down. He was really terrified."

"I can imagine," Jenna said, and Leah knew she could. Her sister Sarah had been in the ICU forever after she'd been hit by a drunk driver.

Taking a seat on the sofa, Jenna tucked her stocking feet beneath her and looked uneasily at Leah, as if suddenly remembering the real reason she'd come.

"Don't think I'm using Zach for an excuse," Leah said tensely, dropping to the edge of a chair. "And for what's it's worth, I haven't told anyone else about you and Peter. Not even Miguel."

"Not Melanie, either?"

"*Especially* not Melanie. Look Jenna, I know I made a huge mistake, and I feel awful about it. I would do anything—*anything*—to make this up to you."

She held her breath, half expecting Jenna to

really tell her off. But something had changed in her friend's expression. She stared wide-eyed at Leah, as if she had just that minute recognized her. Then, to Leah's amazement, she laughed.

"Where have I heard that before?" she asked, still chuckling. "It's true that everything you do comes back to you sooner or later."

"I . . . I don't understand," Leah said, confused but slightly more hopeful.

Jenna shook her head, the smile on her face ironic. "I did the same thing to Caitlin once. It's funny, in a way. I delivered that same speech almost word for word."

"And did she . . . well . . . forgive you?"

Jenna nodded slowly. "Yep. So I guess it's only fair that I forgive you."

"Really?" Leah asked, relieved.

But the smile left Jenna's face as quickly as it had appeared. "I'm already losing my boyfriend. One friend at a time is enough."

"What? No!" Leah moved to the couch to sit beside Jenna. "He didn't break up with you?" She didn't think she could bear it if she'd been responsible for that.

"No," Jenna said miserably, a tear spilling from one blue eye. "But I think I'm going to break up with him."

"Jenna! Why?"

"It's just not working. It's too confusing. I can't . . ." She shook her head. "It would be for the best."

36

"I don't see how. He loves you, Jenna. And I know that you love him."

"I just want things to go back to the way they were before, you know? When we were happy? I want things to go back to normal."

"And you think breaking up will make you happy?"

"No." Jenna was crying harder now, not bothering to hide it. "I don't know. I don't know what to do."

"Then don't decide so fast," Leah urged. "Think about it awhile. Since you're not seeing him at school this week, you have the whole vacation to think it over."

"Not really. There's that Eight Prime meeting on Thursday. And the work party Saturday. What am I supposed to do then? Pretend nothing is wrong?"

"If you have to. I mean, you and Peter know what's going on, and it's no one else's business. Right?"

Jenna wiped away her tears to look Leah in the eye. "Maybe Peter knows what's going on. I don't have a clue."

# Four

"What do you think of this?" Nicole asked, skipping ahead of Melanie in the crowded mall. Walking backward, she struck a pose with her arms. "I was thinking I could start like this—something really dramatic."

"Uh-huh." Melanie glanced nervously at the shoppers all around them. "Or you could just show me later."

Nicole lowered her arms quickly. "I'm not going to *hit* anyone," she said, rebuffed. Did Melanie think she was a klutz?

"I didn't say you were. It's just . . . a few less people looking this way would be all right with me."

"Oh."

Nicole winced apologetically, but she really didn't mind if people checked her out. She was wearing her U.S. Girls contest jeans, the ones she had once barely been able to squeeze into, and a new camisole that was extra cute. A sweater draped over her shoulders made the amount of skin she was showing perfect for the first warm days of spring. She felt good about herself, for once. More than that, she felt like a contender.

"I've got some better ideas for songs," she reported. "I was reading *Cheer!* last night and I copied down this list of music they said every squad should have in its repertoire." Fishing a crumpled paper from her pocket, she handed it to Melanie. "What do you think?"

Melanie's green eyes scanned the list. "No offense, Nicole, but every squad already *does* have these in its repertoire. I think we can be more original. Don't you?"

"I guess," Nicole said, hearing a hint of a whine in her voice. "I mean, sure," she added quickly, "if you know something better. I'll use whatever you say."

Melanie gave her a strange look. "Here's the music store. Let's just see what we find."

Inside, Melanie went through the CDs while Nicole hovered behind her, not daring to offer any more opinions. The last thing she wanted was to lose her coach, especially now, when she was about to make up an original dance. Only the twenty or so girls who made the first cut would try out an original dance—and if Nicole was lucky enough to be one of them, she wanted her dance to be great. In other words, she wanted it choreographed by Melanie.

"What do you think of these guys?" Melanie asked, holding up a CD. "They have a couple of songs I've been considering."

"Yes. Good," Nicole answered immediately. She had never heard of them.

Melanie gave her another of those looks, then set the CD aside and kept flipping. Finally she decided on two songs—one for her and one for Nicole.

"I hope you like that CD," she said as Nicole paid for them both. "I feel kind of weird picking out your music."

"I'll like it," Nicole said firmly. If Melanie said it was good, that was good enough for her.

They were walking out the door when Nicole caught a movement from the corner of her eye. The music store had a protruding front, with recessed alcoves on both sides. In the farther one, only half out of sight, some guy was putting the moves on his girlfriend, making out with her shamelessly. Nicole could only see his back, but even that gave her more information than she needed.

"Geez. Get a room," Melanie muttered, spotting the same thing.

"I know. I mean . . . eew!" Nicole clapped a hand over her mouth as the guy's head turned enough to let her glimpse his profile. Her heart started racing. Her eyes widened with disbelief.

"Is that Kyle Snowden?" Melanie asked. "I thought he was seeing Courtney."

Quickly, before Kyle could notice her, Nicole grabbed Melanie's arm and began pulling her away. "He is," she groaned. "This is terrible!"

"It is kind of low—but of course Kyle's known for that. Personally, I don't know what Courtney wants with the guy. I would have thought she had better taste."

"She does. It's . . . complicated." Nicole hurried toward the mall exit, wanting desperately to get out of there. It wasn't bad enough that Courtney was embarrassing herself with Kyle, now she was embarrassing Nicole, too, just by association.

"Are you going to tell her?" Melanie asked curiously, trailing along behind.

"Tell her?" The mere idea made Nicole weak in the knees. Courtney would be furious. *No, furious isn't strong enough. What comes after furious?* "I don't know if I should."

The automatic doors whirred open, letting them out into the parking lot.

"You have to," Melanie insisted. "I mean, you're her best friend. If you don't tell her, who will?"

"Do you want to?" Nicole asked hopefully.

"No way," Melanie said with a chuckle. "That one's all yours. If it's any consolation, though, tell her she's better off without him."

*Oh, yeah. That's going to make everything smooth.*

Still, Melanie had a point. How devastated could anyone be about losing a guy like Kyle? He was all on

41

the surface, all flash and fake charm. Not only that, but Nicole was convinced that Courtney had never really liked him—she was only using his good looks to make Jeff jealous. Court might be mad that he'd gone behind her back, but Nicole honestly couldn't imagine her spilling too many tears about the whole thing.

By the time she had finally dropped Melanie off and climbed up the stairs to her bedroom, though, Nicole was having second thoughts. Did she really have to tell? Couldn't she just let Courtney find out on her own? She wanted nothing less than to get caught in the middle of *another* of Courtney's romantic disasters.

On the other hand, they were best friends. . . .

*I guess I ought to at least drop some hints.*

The room seemed uncomfortably hot as Nicole dialed the phone. *Maybe she's not home*, she thought hopefully.

But Courtney picked up the call right away. "Hello?"

Something about her voice made Nicole certain her friend was expecting a call from Kyle.

"Hey, Court. What are you doing?" she asked nervously.

"What are *you* doing?" Courtney countered. "I thought you and your best bud, Melanie, were out shopping for pom-poms or something."

"You know she's just trying to help me make the

squad," Nicole said defensively. "And that's supposed to be a secret, remember?"

"And there I go, blabbing to everyone. Oh, wait. The only people listening are you and me."

Nicole bit back a sigh, tired of her friend's sarcasm. "We did go to the mall, though."

"Wow. How exciting."

"We saw Kyle there."

"You did?" Courtney suddenly seemed to find a trip to the mall pretty exciting after all. "Did you talk to him?"

Nicole took a deep breath. "No. He seemed, uh, busy."

"Busy?"

"He was there with someone else. They looked pretty, uh . . . involved."

"Someone who?"

"I didn't get a good look. It was just . . . some . . . girl."

"You saw him with another girl?"

"Yes."

"So what? Did it ever occur to you that she was just a friend or a cousin or something?"

"Um, not really," said Nicole, surprised by Courtney's calm. "That wasn't how it looked."

"Listen, Nicole. I know you don't like Kyle, but this is really immature."

"Excuse me?"

"Kyle and I are doing just fine. Making up sad little stories about him isn't going to break us up."

"Is that what you think?" Nicole demanded, stunned. "That I made this up?"

"I don't know. Maybe not on purpose. But since you obviously can't be impartial, I think it would be better if you and I don't talk about Kyle."

"You think I *want* to talk about Kyle? Sometimes I wonder why I bother talking to you at all!"

Nicole hung up in a huff, completely forgetting she had been afraid that *Courtney* would end up mad. How dare Court believe some guy over her? Especially *that* guy.

"If she wants him, she can have him!" Nicole said, rifling through her dresser for some sweats to practice in. "I have better things to do than make up stories about Kyle Stupid Snowden!"

"Sarah!" Jenna cried, running into the garage to greet her youngest sister.

"You're back! You're home!" Maggie and Allison chorused at her heels.

Caitlin followed a few paces back, an enormous smile on her face.

Mr. Conrad had just driven in, and the van doors weren't even open. Through the side windows, Jenna could see her mother and Sarah on the first bench seat, Sarah waving happily. Jenna yanked the sliding door open, stumbling onto her knees in the van in her haste to be the first to welcome her sister.

"Smooth one, Jenna!" Maggie chortled from behind, but Jenna didn't care. She regained her footing in time to offer Sarah a hand, steadying her until Mr. Conrad came around to lift her to the garage floor.

"Here's her cane," Mrs. Conrad said, setting it up and trying to get Sarah to take it.

"She doesn't need that with all of us here to help her," Mr. Conrad protested.

"You know her physical therapist said she's supposed to walk by herself," Mrs. Conrad said tensely, as if Sarah weren't right there. "She has to practice the movements in order to relearn them."

"I can do it," Sarah said quickly, grabbing the handle of her four-footed cane.

She took a couple of slow, dragging steps toward the interior of the house, her brow furrowing with concentration. Caitlin started to move a helping hand toward Sarah's elbow, then drew it back abruptly, a dismayed look on her face.

"The pudding's still on the stove!" she yelped, running for the kitchen.

Eventually all the Conrads made their way to the kitchen, where Caitlin was scooping slightly curdled chocolate pudding into a cookie-crumb crust. Mr. Conrad pulled out a chair at the table for Sarah, and everyone crowded around.

"We're having your favorite dinner," Maggie told Sarah. "Pizza, salad, and pie."

"Maggie and I made the salad," Allison said importantly.

"Should I put the pizzas in now?" Jenna asked her mother.

"Sorry about the pie," Caitlin apologized, handing Sarah the spatula she'd been using. "It looks a little lumpy, but I think it will taste okay."

Sarah licked the pudding eagerly. "It's good! Is there whipped cream?"

"Of course," Caitlin said with a smile.

She put the pie in the refrigerator to cool while Jenna put the pizzas in the oven. Mrs. Conrad set out drinks and carrot sticks and everyone sat down to talk.

"Now I know I'm really home," Sarah said, taking another lick off the spatula. "They only give you cold pudding in the hospital."

"I want you to get into bed right after dinner, though," Mrs. Conrad said worriedly. "No point overdoing things your first day back."

"Mommm," Sarah groaned. "I'm fine."

"And I thank God for that every day."

Jenna felt her breath catch with her own gratitude. "We ought to have a toast," she said, holding up her soda. "To Sarah! We're glad to have you home."

"To Sarah!" everyone echoed, clinking cans across the table.

"Your mother and I spoke to Officer Rice today," Mr. Conrad said. "The girl who hit Sarah will plead guilty to several counts in exchange for a pre-agreed sentence. That means there won't be a trial, but her license will be suspended a long time, and she'll spend a few months in jail."

"She has to go to jail?" Allison repeated, wide-eyed.

"Now I feel sorry for her," Sarah said guiltily.

"You shouldn't, because she's lucky. She's lucky you didn't . . ." Jenna shook her head, not even wanting to think how close Sarah had come to dying. "No one made her drink and drive. Don't you dare feel bad."

"Jenna's right, honey," Mrs. Conrad said, more gently. "She's actually getting off easy, considering she had an injury hit-and-run on top of a DWI. But she's young, and everyone hopes she'll learn from her mistakes. You shouldn't feel responsible for the punishment she's brought on herself. If she's smart, she *knows* she was lucky—and she'll carry this lesson the rest of her life."

"That's right," Mr. Conrad said, leaning forward to ruffle his youngest's hair. "And now that we don't have to worry about a trial, we can devote all our energy to getting you well."

"I *am* well, Dad."

"Right. But there are those leg exercises to do, and therapy at the hospital. You want to get rid of that cane, don't you?"

Sarah nodded. "Definitely. I will."

"I can help you this week, if you want," Jenna volunteered. "I'm not doing anything. Much," she added defensively as everyone turned to look at her.

"Aren't you and Peter holding that work party up at the lake this week?" Mrs. Conrad asked.

"Well, yeah. But not until Saturday." Jenna rose abruptly from the table, pretending she needed to check on the pizzas. She didn't even want to think about seeing Peter right now. She held her nose close to the oven window, hoping the hot glass might evaporate the tears pooling in her eyes.

"How are the pizzas?" Caitlin asked.

"Almost done. Is Mary Beth coming home Saturday?" Jenna asked, eager to deflect her family's attention.

"Oh, I forgot!" Allison exclaimed. "Mary Beth called while you guys were still at the hospital. She said she wanted to welcome Sarah back."

"Can I call her after dinner, Mom?" Sarah asked.

"We both will," said Mrs. Conrad. "I want to find out when she's planning to get here. Last I heard, it wasn't until Easter morning."

"David's coming first thing Saturday, isn't he, Caitlin?" Jenna asked, her back still to her family.

"I think so," Caitlin said shyly.

"Caitlin has a boyfriend," Allison teased. "Ooh, Caitlin!"

"Caitlin's in *love*!" Maggie one-upped her younger sister.

Jenna turned to see Caitlin blushing furiously but making no attempt to deny it. If anything, she looked kind of pleased.

"I was wondering when we were going to see David again," Mrs. Conrad said. "It's been a while."

"Since Valentine's Day," Caitlin said. "We've been sending e-mails, though. He wanted to come while Sarah was in the hospital, but I asked him to wait until she was out, so I could concentrate on her."

"And now I'm out!" Sarah concluded happily. "Do you like him a whole lot, Cat?"

Caitlin blushed again, her eyes lowered to the table. "Yes," she whispered. "I do."

"I—I'm just going to go wash up before dinner," Jenna said, running for the downstairs bathroom. She barely got the door shut before she burst into tears. Burying her face in a towel, she turned on the water full blast, hoping no one would hear her.

*You're such an idiot to be crying now, with Sarah just come home. Besides, you ought to be happy for Caitlin, not sorry for yourself.*

It was just that now, when everyone else's problems were resolving, hers seemed larger than ever. Sarah didn't need her anymore, and soon Caitlin would be reunited with David. . . .

*And I'll be fighting with Peter. Or breaking up with Peter.* Jenna bunched the towel over her mouth, trying to muffle her sobs.

She knew he was waiting for her to call him, to tell him what she wanted to do. And she wanted to call him—she just didn't know what to say.

Forcing herself to take deep breaths, she finally got enough control to put the towel aside. Then she lowered her face to the sink and splashed her cheeks with cold water over and over again.

*This just isn't how I thought it would be.* When she was a little girl, Jenna had always imagined that falling in love would be so romantic and fun and perfect. *But it isn't that way at all. It's messy and confusing and painful and . . . I just don't get it.*

*How come when you're little, no one ever tells you how much love hurts?*

# Five

"Hey, there he is!" Miguel said excitedly, walking into Zach's room on the children's ward Wednesday afternoon. "I was starting to think you'd packed up your suitcase and left."

"Miguel!" Zach rolled his eyes, but he couldn't hide his pleased smile.

"Well, I'm really glad you didn't," said Miguel, pulling up a chair for a closer look.

It had only been a few days since he'd last seen the boy, but Miguel thought he noticed a change. Zach was still pale, still owl-eyed, but he seemed even thinner, a bit more frail. His brown hair seemed thinner, too, reduced to wispy tufts by the chemotherapy drugs he was taking. He lay amid the IV tubes and wires like a tiny spider in his web.

"You look fine," Miguel lied. "How do you feel?"

"Fine," Zach lied in return.

"You gave us all a thrill, you know. The next time you get bored, you might try something less showy."

Zach giggled, delighted by the idea of all the adults running around in a panic over him. Baby teeth showed in his open mouth, reminding Miguel what a kid he still was.

"I missed you when I was in the ICU," Zach said. "There's no one down there as nice as you."

"I'm sure they're nice. They're just a lot busier than I am." But Miguel felt himself beaming anyway with the joy of being preferred. "I missed you, too. I'm glad you're back."

"Can we play chess today?"

"Sure! I've got the board in the nurses' lounge. I'll just go and get it." Miguel jumped up to make the short trip, but Zach stopped him.

"Are you *positive* you can play this time?" he asked warily. "You don't have to go see all the other kids?"

Miguel winced at the remark, knowing Zach had good reason for asking. Howard, the nurse who had first introduced him to Zach, had later reprimanded him for spending so much time with the boy.

*Yes, but that was only because I was in there so often I was neglecting the other kids*, Miguel reassured himself quickly. *He can hardly object now, when I haven't seen Zach since Friday.*

"Nope. You're my guy today," Miguel said happily. "If you want, we can finish reading that book we've been working on too."

"Howard said he couldn't find that one. He said it must be lost."

Miguel smiled. "That's because I hid it. Did you

think I'd let anyone else take it before we were done?"

Leaving Zachary grinning, Miguel ran off after the chessboard and book. His sneakers skimmed the highly polished floor, gliding along with barely a squeak. His blue scrub top flapped in the breeze he made, flying out behind him. He turned the corner and bolted through the doorway into the nurses' lounge, nearly colliding with Howard and a full cup of coffee.

"Whoa! Ow!" said the nurse, backing up as scalding liquid splashed out onto his hand. "This isn't a racetrack, Miguel."

"Oops. Oops, sorry." Miguel grabbed a handful of napkins off the table and dabbed at Howard's wet hand before kneeling to mop up the drips spattered on the floor.

"We don't usually run around here unless there's an emergency."

"I know. I'm sorry. I just, um . . ."

"Were you just with Zach, by any chance?"

"Well . . . uh . . ."

Surely Howard wasn't going to lecture him about hanging out with Zach today? But when Miguel finally dared to look up, he found Howard smiling, amused.

"It's good to have him back," Howard said. "I've been doing a little skipping around here myself."

"We're going to play chess," said Miguel, emboldened. "And then we're going to read a book. I, uh . . ."

He drew a deep breath and fixed Howard with a challenging gaze. "I might be in there awhile."

Howard laughed. Swirling the remaining coffee around his cup, he blew on it twice, then gulped it down. "Knock yourself out," he said.

"I hope I'm doing this right," Mrs. Rosenthal said anxiously, double-checking the recipe for *haroseth*.

"Is it supposed to look like mud?" Leah asked.

"Actually, yes," Mr. Rosenthal said. "It represents the mortar in the bricks the Hebrew slaves laid for the pharaoh."

"Cheerful," Leah teased.

"I wish your father had given us more notice," Mrs. Rosenthal complained to her husband. "I mean, calling us at the last minute like this, practically dropping in. He can't expect perfection. Can he?"

"He doesn't expect anything," Mr. Rosenthal said, prying the cinnamon out of her hands to fold them in both of his own. "He knows we don't usually make a seder."

It was true. Leah could almost, just barely, remember Passover at her grandparents' house, before her grandmother had died. There had been hours of talk around the table with wine for everyone, even the kids, and singing far into the night. But then her grandfather had moved away and the tradition had been broken. Having been raised Lutheran, Leah's mother now simply lit some candles and made a fancy dinner on the first night of the holiday. Since he had all but abandoned his faith, Leah's father enjoyed the compromise. But this year, at the last minute, Grandfather Rosenthal had called to say he was coming to town so that they could all celebrate Passover together—and he was bringing a guest with him. Leah's mother was doing her best to make everything perfect, but the strain was starting to show.

"What are you serving for dinner?" Mr. Rosenthal asked her.

"Lamb."

He raised an eyebrow. "Lamb?"

"It's not supposed to be lamb?"

"It doesn't have to be."

"Where else was I supposed to get a lamb shank bone for the seder plate?" she asked testily.

"Lamb is fine," he said quickly.

"Leah, how about arranging those flowers and putting them on the table with the candles?" Mrs. Rosenthal directed, pointing to a waxed-paper-wrapped bundle on the counter.

The next hour went by in a flurry of preparation. Leah's father took over setting the table, while Leah watched with interest. At the head of the table, where her grandfather would sit, the seder plate was placed. In addition to the shank bone and *haroseth*, it held celery, freshly grated horseradish, a hard-boiled egg, and a dish of salt water, all symbols with special meaning to Passover. Next to that, another plate held three sheets of matzoh. The rest of the table was set as for any fancy dinner, except that there were wineglasses and additional dishes of salt water for everyone, and a small book on each dinner plate, a Haggadah, to guide the telling of the Passover story. An extra wineglass for the prophet Elijah was placed near the center of the table, and lastly her father put a pillow in her grandfather's chair, to show that they were free people, eating at their leisure.

"Is that everything?" Leah asked as her father stood back to survey his work.

"I think so, as far as the table goes. There's more, of course, if we were really going to do things right. We should have cleaned the entire house and gotten rid of all the bread and everything else that isn't kosher for Passover. My mom even had special dishes just for—"

The doorbell rang, interrupting them.

"Joe!" Leah's mother called from the kitchen. "Can you get that? I'll be out in a minute."

But before her father could react, Leah ran to open the door.

"Grandpa!" she cried, throwing herself into his open arms. Bald except for a gray fringe and tall like Leah, the senior Mr. Rosenthal hadn't lost his strength. He lifted her feet off the ground with the force of his bear hug.

"You are beautiful!" he declared. "I do good work."

"And you don't mind taking the credit," Leah returned, laughing as he set her down.

"I'd be crazy not to." Turning his head, he urged the woman at his side forward into the doorway. "Leah, I'd like you to meet Nadia Gold."

"Nice to meet you," Leah said, recognizing the name at once. Her grandfather's mystery guest was the widow from his building, the one he'd eaten latkes with at Hanukkah!

"Please, come in," Leah's father said, reaching to shut the door and take their coats.

Mrs. Gold was a small, white-haired woman, almost frail in comparison with her date. Her smile was warm and ready, though, and her brown eyes sparkled with good humor.

"I hope our being here today isn't inconvenient," she said as Mrs. Rosenthal came bustling out of the kitchen. "I know we didn't give you much notice."

"Not at all!" Leah's mother protested, as if she hadn't just been moaning about the same thing. "We're delighted to have you both."

They sat in the living room for the first half hour, talking as the shadows lengthened toward sundown. From the conversation, Leah gathered that her grandfather had been seeing a lot of Mrs. Gold over the last few months—a development that gave her a secret thrill, especially since Mrs. Gold seemed so nice. Leah's grandfather had never remarried after her grandmother died, and Leah had always hated the idea of his living alone in another state. She knew he had lots of friends there, but friends weren't nearly as good as a girlfriend.

"They're so *sweet!*" Leah gushed, cornering her mother alone in the kitchen. "Do you think they're going to get married? Maybe they'll move back here!"

Mrs. Rosenthal smiled and rolled her eyes heavenward. "Rushing things a bit, aren't you? Here, help me take this wine to the table, and then it's time to get started."

Leah had read about the symbolism of the seder in the course of her religious pursuits, but she didn't remember the details, only that it memorialized the flight of the Hebrews from Egypt and their resulting freedom. But from the opening blessing at the lighting of the candles, she felt a strange sense of history repeating itself. The seder was a retelling of history, of course, but her feeling went deeper than that. Her grandfather poured everyone the first of four cups of wine, and as he recited the kiddush, Leah felt an unexpectedly deep connection—with him, with her father, with the countless generations that had lived between her and those who had fled Egypt. The ceremony wasn't just history, it was *her* history. By the time her father motioned for her to dip her piece of celery into the salt water—symbols of new life and tears—she found her hand was trembling.

Her grandfather broke the middle matzoh on the plate, ceremonially inviting the hungry and needy to celebrate Passover with them. Then came the reading of the four questions, asking why things were done a special way that night. Traditionally asked in Hebrew by the youngest child, the questions were posed by Leah reading English translations from the Haggadah. Her father followed up with the Hebrew, making Leah wish that someone had taught her the language, the way that he'd been taught.

Then came the tale of the Jewish exodus—the pharaoh's stubbornness and the ten plagues that were sent to move him. With the telling of each plague, everyone dipped a finger into his or her wineglass, spilling a drop of wine out of sadness at the memory. The last and most horrible plague was recounted, the death of the firstborn Egyptians, and the table fell silent.

Then, as if on secret cue, Leah's father, her grandfather, and Mrs. Gold burst out singing in Hebrew. It was a happy song, a grateful song. Leah could tell even without understanding the words. She listened raptly, soaking up every note, and afterward, when her grandfather went to wash his hands before dinner, Leah used the moment to whisper to her father.

"Next year, I want to do this again," she told him, moved enormously. "But I want to do the whole thing—the cleaning, the special dishes, the Hebrew. Next year, I want to do it all."

"A lot of people noticed our ad in the newspaper, and I think we can probably expect a pretty big crowd this Saturday," Peter said at the Eight Prime meeting on Thursday. "Especially if this weather holds."

Jesse squirmed impatiently in the armchair he'd snagged in the Altmanns' living room. They'd already been there half an hour, and as far as he could see they hadn't accomplished a thing. All he'd heard was a lot of jawing on Peter's part without any actual assignments being made.

"So what do we have to do to get ready?" Miguel asked, obviously thinking along the same lines. "I mean, what specifically?"

"My family is going to be there early—probably by seven," Peter answered. "It would be great if everyone else could be there before nine, because that's when things will get busy. We're going to need as many shovels, rakes, and saws as we can get, plus hammers, nails, and all the building tools. I don't think there's any way to plan more specifically. Just bring as many things as you can—and make sure your name is on anything you want back."

"It's going to seem weird working without Ben," said Leah. "Who'll provide the entertainment?"

"I can do just fine without that type of entertainment," Nicole said. "We should be *glad* he's spending the week at his grandma's house, where nobody can get hurt."

"Ben wasn't too glad," said Peter. "His folks sprang it on him at the last minute."

"Well, I hope he doesn't think we're helpless without him," Melanie said, "because I'm pretty sure we'll muddle through."

Jesse snickered. Ben Pipkin, the eighth member of their group, was more uncoordinated than all Three Stooges rolled into one. Melanie started to glance his way, and Jesse sat up straighter, but before they made eye contact she turned back to face Peter.

*What is up with her?* he wondered, frustrated. All meeting long, he'd been trying to catch her eye, but his entire end of the room seemed invisible to her. She was practically close enough to touch, sitting on the couch with Leah and Miguel, but her gaze had been turned toward the chair Peter was yakking from the whole time. Nicole and Jenna had the love seat next to that, so most of the action was down that way, but still . . . it seemed like Melanie could at least have *looked* at him.

"What are we doing about food and drinks out there?" asked Miguel. "Are we bringing anything?"

"The first thing I'm going to do is try to tap into the water supply," said Peter. "If we can get a hose hooked up, then at least everyone will have water to drink. If you want something else, bring it. And don't forget to pack a lunch."

Jesse's attention wandered as more, similarly unimportant, questions were asked and answered. Melanie was wearing a fuzzy white sweater and a red heart-shaped stone on a chain. He leaned farther forward, hoping to catch her peripheral vision.

"Are there going to be snakes out there?" Nicole asked.

*Just a little farther . . .*

Peter's latest treasury report fell off Jesse's lap, fluttering to the floor. He and Melanie bent to retrieve it simultaneously, nearly bumping heads.

"Oops." She giggled softly as she handed it to him.

His fingers brushed hers, the coolness of her skin sending a jolt up his arm. For a moment the rest of the room was forgotten. They were still bent low, their faces so close he thought he could see his reflection in her eyes. He smiled tentatively, and the answering smile she gave him nearly took his breath away. His lips were just inches from hers. . . . She almost seemed to be thinking the same thing. . . .

And then she sat up abruptly, turning her eyes back to Peter.

*What was that?* Jesse wondered, slouching back in his chair. *Talk about mixed signals!* Had she been checking him out? Or was she just being polite?

He didn't have a clue.

*Maybe it's time to be more obvious. Drop a couple of hints and see what she says. I could offer to drive her home. . . .*

"Are we done here?" he asked, standing up. "I think we've covered everything twice by now."

Peter looked surprised but rose to his feet too. "I guess so. This is just one of those things you can't plan completely until you get there."

"I'm sure it will be fine," Leah said. "Besides, how can we lose? It's not like we have a bunch of money invested in this one. The whole idea is genius."

Jesse puffed up a bit but managed not to remind them whose idea it had been.

Jenna closed her ever-present spiral pad. Leah and Miguel stood up. Jesse suddenly realized that if he didn't act fast Melanie would be gone before he had talked to her.

"So," he said quickly, dropping back into his chair. "How's your vacation been so far?"

She smiled slightly, as if surprised to be asked. "All right. Yours?"

He shook his head. "I've had more exciting weeks."

"If excitement's the criteria," she said, laughing, "I might have to change my answer. I was working on the assumption that anything's better than school."

"Okay. You have me there."

She was smiling again, and he felt a grin on his face too. There *was* something about the way she was looking at him.

"Do you need a ride home?" he blurted out.

"Well..."

Her cheeks dimpled. She lowered her eyes, a sweep of black lashes against pink skin. He was sure she was going to say yes.

"No, that's okay," she said. "Nicole'll run me home. In fact, I think she's waiting for me now. I'd better go."

Jesse watched in amazement as Melanie jumped to her feet, interrupted Nicole's conversation with Leah, and dragged her friend out the door, a diet soda still clutched in her hand.

*She's crazy!* he thought. *Or she's trying to make* me *crazy. Does that girl like me, or not?*

Jesse shook his head. *A guy would need a crystal ball.*

# Six

"Well, this stinks," Jenna said, throwing her diary to one side and falling backward onto her bed. "I *hate* this stupid vacation!"

At least if they were at school she'd have a chance to run into Peter by accident.

*Not that it would probably do me much good.*

The night before, at the Eight Prime meeting, he had barely looked at her. He had managed a chilly hello, and that was about all. She couldn't even remember what she'd said back to him. Maybe she'd only nodded.

"This is torture!" she groaned, muffling herself with her pillow even though there was no one around to hear her. Her father and Caitlin were at work, her mother had taken Sarah to physical therapy, and Maggie and Allison were out with friends. "I should have said something!"

But what? She had gone to the meeting hoping that something would occur to her when she saw him. But it hadn't. In fact, she had sat on the love seat with Nicole, getting more tongue-tied by the second. Every time she'd looked up from taking the meeting notes, it had seemed all she could see was Melanie Andrews, blond, petite, and beautiful enough to make Jenna feel like crying.

*Why did she have to kiss Peter in the first place?* Jenna wondered unhappily. *If she hadn't, none of this would have happened. Peter and I would still be together, and everything would be fine.*

*Of course, if I hadn't been so completely blinded by my crush on Miguel, it wouldn't have happened either,* she thought with a sigh. The last few days had given her plenty of time to think about things from Peter's perspective. She took responsibility now for the mistakes she had made, and she was more than willing to apologize to Peter. But as far as getting over it . . .

*Maybe if Melanie were less pretty, or less drooled over by every guy at school. Maybe if I hadn't always kind of suspected they liked each other. Or maybe if I just weren't so insecure!*

Jenna knew she wasn't being reasonable, but there was no way she could honestly say she was over the kiss those two had shared. She didn't think she ever would be.

Every glimpse of Melanie just brought it up all over again.

"Perfect!" Nicole declared, finishing a run-through of her original dance in her room Friday morning. She could have done all the moves full-size if she'd gone down to the basement, but better to be cramped than spied on by her weasel of a sister. "I think I've really got it."

She and Melanie had just completed the choreography on their dances the day before, and Nicole had been practicing all morning, wanting to make sure she didn't forget anything. It was amazing enough that Melanie had helped her so much the first time—she might not want to do it again if Nicole didn't remember what she'd been taught.

*She said I was doing good, though,* Nicole thought happily, stopping the CD to recue her music. *The last time I ran through it yesterday, she said it was coming together.*

Of course, she'd never look as good as Melanie. Even with as much effort as she'd put into helping Nicole choreograph her own routine, Melanie still had a better one. Or maybe it was just the person performing it. As hard as Nicole tried to copy every move that Melanie made, she couldn't seem to capture the same flair. Melanie was a lot smaller than she was, for one thing; what looked sharp and sassy on her didn't always translate to Nicole's longer arms and legs. But it was more than that. It was Melanie's smile, her precision, her confidence. . . .

*It doesn't matter,* Nicole thought quickly. *Melanie was always sure to make the squad again, so getting insecure about her is a total waste of time. Better to focus on being her.*

Nicole pushed the Play button on her stereo, ran to hit her opening pose, and began her dance again. *Snap those arms, Nicole*, she could almost hear Melanie saying. *Keep it crisp!*

She imagined herself flowing through the moves, sharp but smooth, as graceful as a martial artist. Since she couldn't hit every position to the fullest in that confined space, she focused on hitting them right on the beat. She was about to launch into her favorite part when a sudden loud knock on her bedroom door nearly gave her a heart attack.

"Heather! I told you to leave me alone," she shouted, bounding toward the noise. But before she could get there the door flew open.

"Got that turned up loud enough?" Courtney yelled. "Geez, give my eardrums a break." She lowered the volume herself. "You might want to open a window, too," she advised, waving a hand in front of her face.

Nicole grudgingly dropped her practice pom-poms and cracked her window open. As surprised as she was by Courtney's unscheduled appearance, she was even more irritated to be interrupted in the middle of her dance. "It's warm in here on purpose," she said testily, "to keep my muscles loose."

Courtney sat down on the bed, a mocking smile on her face. "I wasn't talking about the temperature. I thought you were never supposed to let them see you sweat. Or smell you, I should say."

"Very funny." Nicole grabbed a towel from her bathroom and wiped herself down, even though she was pretty sure Courtney was making things up. After all, messing with people was what Courtney lived for. "So what are you doing here anyway?"

"What's the matter?" Courtney asked. "Am I cutting into your pom-pom time?"

"I thought you were mad at me, actually."

"I was," Courtney admitted. "But it turns out . . . well . . . you might be kind of right about Kyle seeing other people."

"I know I am," said Nicole, still too annoyed to soften her answer. "What finally clued you in?"

Courtney shrugged. "I asked him and he told me."

"He *told* you?"

Courtney made a face. "You don't need to sound so indignant. Kyle and I don't have one of those possessive kind of things. Besides, I never wanted it to be permanent."

Courtney smiled, but there was a reined-in quality to her voice that told Nicole how hurt she really was. Despite their earlier fight, Nicole felt a rush of sympathy for her friend. She perched on the end of the bed, afraid to get too close just in case she *didn't* smell good.

"I'm sorry, Court," she ventured. "But you're better off without him."

"No doubt."

"So you're going to dump him, then?" Nicole asked hopefully.

Courtney snorted. "Hardly. At least not until I replace him."

"But—"

"Let's talk about something else. What are we doing this weekend?"

"This weekend? Uh . . . Eight Prime is having that work party up at the lake, remember?"

"The God Squad *again*?" Courtney whined. "Between them and your stupid cheerleading tryouts, I've barely seen you for weeks."

"Whose fault is that? It's not like you've been sitting home alone."

"Okay, fine. Don't remind me." Courtney inspected the chipped polish on her nails. "Maybe I'll come with you."

"Right!" scoffed Nicole. "You want to rake old leaves and wade in knee-deep muck."

Courtney rolled her eyes. "I'm sure there's something else I could do. What will you be doing?"

"I don't know. Maybe painting the old shed."

"Well, you're not going to paint it all by yourself. I might as well help you."

Nicole's heart sped up. Courtney was serious.

"Oh, I don't think you want to come," she said

quickly. "You don't even like Jenna and Peter, and . . . and . . ."

"And what?" Courtney said suspiciously.

"I thought helping people was against your religion," Nicole said desperately.

"What?" Courtney gave her a disbelieving look. "Helping isn't against my religion, *religion* is against my religion. I helped at the haunted house, didn't I?"

"Well, yes. But I thought that was only because *Jeff* wanted to." The moment Jeff's name left her lips, Nicole knew she had made a mistake. Too much emphasis, maybe even a trace of fear . . .

"That's it, isn't it?" Courtney demanded, pointing an accusing finger. "Jeff's going to be there tomorrow. *With that girl!*"

Nicole cringed. "Might. He *might* be there. You don't want to go, Courtney. If they do show up, it'll just be weird."

But there was a sparkle in Courtney's green eyes that hadn't been there a moment before. "Oh, I'm going," she said, a slow, wicked smile on her lips. "I am so there."

# Seven

Jenna hurried down the dirt pathway into the old Boy Scouts' camp Saturday, hoping to catch Peter alone. She was there so early the mist was still rising off the lake, but she'd seen Peter's Toyota in the parking lot, so she knew he was around.

*I'll just talk to him now. Before everyone else gets here. And before I lose my nerve.*

She had practiced what she wanted to say over and over the night before, but now she barely remembered any of it. What parts she *could* remember sounded ridiculous. But she had to say something. She had let things go on too long already.

A clearing opened before her, thick with old leaves and dead wood. The broken-down shack she'd seen in the photographs blended into the brush on the far side, but Peter was near the center, his gloved hands digging through the compost beneath a single huge oak tree. He didn't notice her, so she walked toward him, her hiking boots crunching through the dry vegetation.

He looked up as she approached, alerted by the noise. Rising slowly, he wiped his hands on his faded jeans.

"You here all by yourself?" he asked with obvious surprise. "I thought Caitlin was coming."

"She'll be here later, after she finishes walking her dogs." Jenna looked around them but saw only deserted woods. "Your family's not here?"

"My parents are waiting for David. They'll all be here any time."

She needed to hurry, then. Taking a deep breath, Jenna plunged ahead.

"Peter, I just want to say I'm sorry. You have no idea how awful I feel." Her voice was shaking so badly she could barely keep going, but she was determined to apologize. "I knew that maybe I wasn't being fair—that's why I kept my mouth shut. But I never thought I was *lying*. I mean, it just never occurred to me." She had to stop to breathe, a deep, shuddering inhalation.

"It's okay," Peter said, his eyes softening with sympathy. "We probably both wish certain things had never happened, but at least it's finally over."

He reached to fold her into a hug, but she stepped backward before he could.

"No," she said, shaking her head. "I *am* sorry—I really mean that. But I'm still not over it. I try to be, but I just can't seem to forget. Especially not with Melanie around everywhere I look."

Peter dropped his arms. "Don't tell me you're mad at Melanie now."

"I'm not *mad* at her, Peter, I just—"

"If you are, you'll just be losing a friend for no reason. Melanie never would have done anything if she'd thought you and I were together."

The way he said it, with such conviction, made a chill run down to her feet. He spoke as if he knew Melanie's mind like his own, and in that instant, Jenna *did* feel the sharp, cold fear of losing a friend. But the friend she feared losing was Peter.

"Could we break up and still be friends?" she blurted out. "I mean, would you still like me if we did?"

"You want to break up?" he asked, stunned.

"No. I don't *want* to, but—"

"Then don't," he said, taking one of her arms to better stare into her eyes. "We can get through this, Jenna. Just give us another chance."

"If—if you think so," she said dubiously. She wanted to believe him, more than anything, but—

"Hey! There you guys are." David Altmann's voice broke in on them. "I was starting to think I was lost."

Peter let go of her and looked toward his brother, confused. "Where are Mom and Dad?"

"Back at the car. Mom decided to bring a ton of food and drinks, and Dad's got all his tools to un-load." David held up Eight Prime's folded card table. "If you tell me where you want this, Mom'll have a place to put the refreshments."

Peter hesitated, his eyes darting back and forth between Jenna and his brother. He clearly had more to say, but how could they finish the conversation now, with David standing right there? Jenna felt tears rise up to burn behind her lids, and she honestly didn't know if they were from frustration or relief.

"I—I'm going to help your mother," she said, turning and running away. She didn't want Peter to see her crying. She didn't want anyone else to see her at all. Detouring off the path and into the woods, she wondered what was wrong with her. She loved Peter. And he had just practically begged her not to break up with him.

Shouldn't she be happy?

"Stay back, Amy. You're going to get wet."

Six-year-old Amy Robbins took a step away from the edge of the lake, her little rubber boots making sucking sounds in the mud. Her curls formed a bobbing brown halo around her face. "*You're* getting wet," she pointed out, pursing disapproving lips.

"Not on purpose." Melanie reached out as far as she could, and with a final lunge managed to get a grip on the dead tree branch she'd been fishing for. Icy water lapped at the toes of her boots, but she backed up the sloping shore before it could soak through the leather. "There!" she said, dragging the waterlogged branch up behind her. "We can add that to the pile."

"You want me to take it over?" Amy asked eagerly.

Melanie smiled at the thought of the little girl moving the heavy branch by herself. "You can help me. Grab on and we'll pull it together."

There were other people gathering brush along the shore, but Melanie had been working alone with Amy, keeping an eye on her while Mr. Robbins helped repair the old shed. There were other Junior Explorers there with their parents too, all of Eight Prime except Ben, their friends and family members, and many total strangers who had read about the event in the paper. The turnout was so tremendous, in fact, that it was hard to find things to work on that someone else wasn't already taking care of. Melanie and Amy dragged their branch up over the rise and started walking into the central clearing, only to discover that the crowd had grown even larger.

"Look at all these people!" Melanie gasped. "Where did they all come from?"

"I see my daddy!" Amy cried, dropping her end of the branch to scamper off.

Melanie dragged the dead wood the rest of the way to the big central oak, where Chris Hobart was using a chain saw to cut up the larger pieces for people to take home as firewood.

"I can't believe this!" she said to Peter. "You'd think we were building a hotel out here."

"We almost could," Peter said proudly. "We have more stuff than we can possible use, and probably more people, too. This place is going to look fantastic."

"Most of the brush is cleared off the shore now, if you want to get people started on the dock."

He nodded. "My brother, David, is going to head that up with my dad. There are a few people here who brought waders, and my dad thinks the old supports are still good. With all the wood we have . . ." Peter's grin spoke for itself.

"Now all we need is a boat," Melanie concluded.

"I think we have enough wood for that, too," Chris quipped, walking over to take her branch.

A moment later the chain saw roared to life, rendering conversation impossible. Melanie stood beside Peter, watching the barely controlled chaos around them. A group of Junior Explorers—Danny, Elton, Lisa, and Cheryl—were playing tag in the middle of the clearing, threatening to overturn Mrs. Altmann's refreshment table any second. Jenna was leading a rake brigade of fifteen energetic adults; her sister Caitlin was helping David Altmann load the resulting leaves, rocks, and pine cones into wheelbarrows and roll them off into the woods. A small mob swarmed around the old shack, sanding the weathered walls and setting in new windows. There were even people up on ladders making a sheet-metal roof. Melanie saw Leah and Miguel over there, as well as Nicole and Courtney. To Melanie's surprise, a gorgeous young brunette seemed to be running the show, shouting orders to much older men.

The chain saw switched off abruptly, allowing voices to be heard again.

"Who's the babe in the painter pants?" Melanie asked, curious.

Peter followed her finger. "Sabrina something. Miguel used to work for her dad."

"She seems to know what she's doing."

"Yeah. I think she ran Miguel's work crew. Her dad's here somewhere too. He's going to do the plumbing for the drinking fountain soon. It'll be right next to that stake." Peter pointed to a stick flying a piece of construction flagging just a few feet behind them.

"We ought to be nearly ready for that," Chris said, joining the conversation again. "Most of the big wood has already been cleared, and there's no reason we can't take the branches somewhere else if we find more. Let's start putting together the things we'll need for the fountain."

"Good idea." Peter began to walk off, but Melanie stopped him before he could get very far.

"Have you, uh, seen Jesse lately? I know he was here earlier, but . . ."

"Last I saw Jesse, he was talking about finding a fallen tree we could make into more benches. He went that way, I think." Peter nodded toward a narrow trailhead before taking off in search of Sabrina's father.

Melanie peered up the path, hoping for a glimpse of Jesse, but all she could see was the edge of the woods. Was he out there somewhere? If so, would she be able to find him?

Ever since he'd shown up at the lake that morning, Jesse had been working by himself, moving farther to the fringes as more and more people arrived. Melanie had almost joined him a dozen times. He looked so cute, and lonely . . . and available. Only the fear of being made foolish had helped her stay away. Then Amy had shown up and taken her mind off him for a while. But now Melanie was on her own again. . . .

*If you follow him into the woods, it's going to be pretty obvious you're out there looking for him. What else would you be doing?*

Even so, she couldn't resist taking a few steps in that direction. Everyone was so busy that no one was likely to notice if she slipped off for a few minutes.

*I'll just hurry out and hurry back*, she decided, beginning to walk more purposefully. *I can always say I was getting claustrophobic in the crowd*.

The trees closed over her head as she hustled up the path, their branches budding with new growth. Pine needles crunched under her boots, adding to the smell of sap in the air. Considering all the places Jesse could have struck off the trail, she almost didn't expect to find him, but she'd been walking less than five minutes when she spotted him coming back down the hill. His jacket was open, his hands stuffed into his jeans pockets. A shock of brown hair fell over his eyes, making her heart nearly break with longing.

"Hey, Melanie," he greeted her carelessly. "What are you doing here?"

"Peter said you were out here looking for a tree," she answered, trying to keep her voice light. "Did you plan on carrying that back yourself, or could you use a little help?"

He threw back his head and laughed. "That's a picture: you, carrying the other end of a tree."

"You don't think I can?" she asked, flexing a biceps.

"I'd like to see you try, that's for sure."

His blue eyes raked her over, the way they'd used to. Her breath caught in her chest. Suddenly she ached to reach forward, pull him to her by the fronts of his open jacket, and kiss him the way he'd once kissed her. It had been New Year's Eve, and Jesse had schemed all night just to get her alone.

Did he even still remember?

*Of course he doesn't. If he did, would he be hiding up here in the woods when he knows I'm down there by myself?*

Back when Jesse had wanted her, he'd stuck so close there was barely room for her shadow.

"I—I have to go. I just remembered something," she blurted out, spinning around on the path. Before he could say a word, she rushed back toward the clearing.

Coming out looking for Jesse had been a bad idea. Letting herself even *think* about Jesse had been a bad idea.

She'd had her chance. She'd blown it. It was over.

The sooner she went out with someone else, the better.

"Oh, Jeff, you're *so* funny," Courtney mimicked Hope in a voice that dripped acid. "Can you believe that phony witch?"

"Can you keep your voice down?" Nicole countered in a frantic whisper. "They're going to hear you!"

"So what?"

Courtney shot her ex and his replacement redhead

an unbelievably nasty look. The pair was painting together on the other end of the shed, Hope looking cute in a white T-shirt and faded jeans, her hair slicked into a ponytail with a green scarf tied around it. Jeff's eyes had been so glued to her ever since they'd arrived that Nicole wasn't even sure he'd noticed Courtney's presence.

*We can only hope*, she thought, looking nervously from Jeff and Hope back to Courtney.

In contrast to Hope's simple outfit, Courtney had gone for drama, showing a complete disregard for the fact that they were supposed to be there to work. Her fuzzy black sweater clung to her full chest and stopped an inch above her red hip-huggers, exposing a strip of creamy white skin. Unlike Hope, with her smooth ponytail, Courtney had curled her bright hair into a mane that tumbled around her shoulders, catching every ray of light.

"She looks like something out of *Happy Days*," Courtney said, still glaring. "No wonder you'd rather hang out with me than with those guys!"

Nicole's smile felt stiff on her face. Did Courtney really think she was hanging out with her to avoid Hope?

*I could care less about Hope. It's Guy I want to avoid.*

She glanced at Hope and Jeff again, just in time to see Guy rejoin them with another bucket of paint. He looked over immediately, as if he felt her gaze upon him. Their eyes met for just a moment before

Nicole glanced away, her heart pounding. The last thing she wanted was for him to come over.

She had spoken to him briefly when he'd first shown up with Hope and Jeff in tow.

"I'm not going to be able to work with you guys," she had whispered hurriedly. "Courtney's here, and I'd better stay with her."

"What? Why can't we all work together?" he'd asked with his usual cluelessness.

"Yeah," Nicole had snorted. "Right. Listen, you just keep Jeff away from us, and I'll do my best to return the favor."

"I don't understand. You said it would be fine if they came."

"I didn't know Courtney was coming then, did I?" she'd retorted. "Look, just take my word for it. You don't want her around Hope."

Since then Guy had kept his distance, but Nicole could tell he wasn't happy about the situation. She'd caught him looking her way again and again, almost as if he missed her.

*I hope he does,* she thought spitefully, slapping more green paint on the wall she and Courtney were supposed to be covering. *It would serve him right.*

"Hey! Watch the splatters!" Courtney complained, backing up. "If you get paint on this outfit I won't be happy."

"I don't know why you wore that in the first place. I told you we were going to be painting."

"I didn't know we were going to be painting *me*," Courtney returned sarcastically. "How about paying more attention? Nobody had better say that little priss down there did a better job than we did."

Nicole smoothed out her brushstrokes, wishing she were anywhere else. With as many volunteers as had turned out, Eight Prime didn't even need her—and she certainly had better things to do.

*I should be home practicing my original dance*, she thought. *Not wasting my time on a camp that's not even going to open until summer.*

"I ought to go over and give them both a piece of my mind," Courtney said, glowering toward the other end of the shed.

*Not to mention the stomachache I'm getting.*

Nicole looked up to see Jeff and Hope sharing a private moment without their brushes, laughing under a dogwood tree a few feet back from the shed. They both had splashes of paint on their clothes, but they didn't seem to mind. Jeff leaned against the tree trunk with one strong arm, his eyes devouring Hope.

"He's faking, I know it," Courtney insisted. "He's just acting that way to make me jealous."

*If that's an act, he's wasting his talent. He ought to be in Hollywood.*

"Where's Guy?" Nicole asked, suddenly realizing he was missing.

"I don't know. He took off a couple of minutes ago."

"Do you think he left?"

"Do you think I care?" Courtney put down her paintbrush to better scowl at Jeff.

*I don't care either*, Nicole told herself, ignoring the unpleasant feeling in her gut. If Guy wanted to leave without saying good-bye, that was fine with her. In fact, it would be a relief.

So why did she keep looking over her shoulder at the path to the parking lot? It wasn't that she cared. It was just . . .

*He wouldn't really leave without saying good-bye. Would he?*

She was on the verge of making an excuse to go see if his car was still there when Guy reappeared on the path. Instead of feeling relief, however, Nicole felt her heart nearly stop at the sight. He was carrying his guitar.

"Well, well. What have we got here?" Courtney asked, spotting him at the same time. "Wait, don't tell me. We're having a sing-along! Gee, Nicole. You sure can pick the cool ones."

"He happens to be a good singer," Nicole retorted defensively, but inside she was dying a hundred deaths. She hadn't admitted to Courtney that she and Guy were having problems, but if he was going to embarrass her in front of so many people she didn't even want to admit that she knew him. She watched surreptitiously as Guy sat on one of the two split-log benches facing the new flagpole. Out behind him the cold lake glittered as he tuned up, his russet head bent over the strings. People who were working in the area began to glance his way, and a moment later Jenna walked over and sat beside him on the long bench.

"This just keeps getting better," Courtney sniped, no longer even pretending to work. "Here comes 'Jesus Loves Me.' "

Nicole closed her eyes and pretended she wasn't there. She was sure Guy wouldn't play anything nearly that juvenile, but she was also pretty sure he would play a Christian song, which Courtney was sure to ridicule. Guy's band, Trinity, wrote its own music and had even performed at the Hearts for God rally in Los Angeles. It wasn't that Nicole didn't *like* his music, it was just that there was a time and a place for everything—and this was neither. Sure enough, the first song he started playing was one Nicole had heard before, not only in L.A. but also in Sarah Conrad's hospital room.

Guy's voice floated out to her, as strong and on key as always. Nicole tried not to let the fact that he could really sing cloud the issue of how much he was embarrassing her. But then a soprano voice joined in, as sweet as Guy's was strong, and Nicole's eyes flew open in surprise.

Jenna was singing too.

Nicole knew she had heard the song before, but

she'd had no idea that Jenna could sing the way she was singing now. She sounded like a rock star, or a diva, or an angel. People stopped what they were doing to wander over and listen to the impromptu duet.

"Maybe after this we can roast marshmallows and make s'mores," Courtney said, but there was an awe in her voice that she couldn't quite hide.

The song came to a close, ending on the sweetest of notes, and the crowd that had gathered burst into spontaneous applause. People were whistling and calling for encores. Almost without realizing she was moving, Nicole wandered forward toward the benches, weaving her way through the other onlookers.

"You guys sound great together!" Leah was congratulating Jenna. "Wow!"

"You ought to be a steady duo," a stranger said. "I'll bet you could play weddings."

"Thanks," Jenna said shyly, "but Guy already has a band."

"Then you ought to join it," the man insisted. "They'd be crazy not to ask you."

Guy gave Jenna a speculative look. "We haven't been playing much lately. But maybe, the next time we get together . . ."

Jenna blushed and shrugged. "Yeah. Maybe."

Nicole pushed her way the last few feet to the very front of the crowd, but Guy was so busy staring that he didn't even notice her. He was gazing at Jenna like an admiration society of one, as if she were the only person there.

And all of a sudden Nicole was jealous—not just a little jealous either, but completely, searingly overcome. In an instant she understood exactly how Courtney felt.

*Maybe I'm not quite as ready to give Guy up as I thought.*

Leah rested a hand on Miguel's leg as they sat side by side on the worn wooden bench, their backs to the lake. The sun had just dipped behind the hills, bathing the camp in shadow, but Leah wasn't cold. The glow of that day's accomplishments felt like a warmth inside her.

"Happy?" she asked Miguel, looking at the clearing.

He put an arm around her shoulders. "It looks good, doesn't it?"

"It looks great."

The clearing, all but deserted now except for Eight Prime, had been raked down to hard-packed dirt, ready for baseball, soccer, or whatever else the kids dreamed up. Beside the central oak tree, a drinking fountain and sink had turned into a redwood sculpture under Chris's creative direction, and a half ring of three picnic tables stood ready for lunchtime or crafts. The old shed looked new in the failing light, with its fresh pine-green paint, and glass glinting in the windows. Inside, the floor had been fitted with a strong new layer of plywood, shelves and cupboards had been built, and the walls had been painted white. There was a big new storage closet out back now too, to house the sports equipment. Adding that had been Sabrina's idea, when she'd realized how much wood they had left.

When Sabrina had first shown up, Leah had been anything but glad to see her. For a while it had even seemed like the girl was going out of her way to get Miguel's attention. But Miguel had ignored her except to follow orders, and now Leah had to admit that Sabrina was a construction wizard—just like Miguel had always claimed. She had been a fool to be so jealous.

"Sabrina and her dad were a huge help," Leah said, turning to look over her shoulder at the new dock. Small but solid, it would make a great swimming platform come summer. "I feel silly now for making such a big deal about you working with her."

"Uh-huh. Look, here comes Peter."

Miguel took his arm off her shoulders to point across the clearing. Peter and Chris were walking over with Jesse, who was carrying the cash box. Putting two fingers in his mouth, Peter blew a piercing whistle, summoning everyone to the benches. Nicole and Melanie came out from behind the shed. Down on the beach, Caitlin and David appeared from around a point and started walking toward the group. Jenna appeared last of all, stepping out of the woods by herself.

"Okay, everyone gather round," Peter called. "I have some fantastic news!"

Soon they were all standing in a huddle by the newly erected flagpole, crowding close against the growing cold.

"First of all, we owe Jesse a round of applause or something. Look at this place!" Peter gestured at the pristine campground. "The Junior Explorers will have a blast out here."

Leah clapped happily along with the others.

"Not only that," Peter continued, "we got some great donations. There's over a hundred dollars in the cash box, all those supplies in the shed, and somebody gave us a volleyball net. And there's more."

Peter looked around the group, a growing smile on his face. "I didn't want to say this before, but Chris isn't going to be able to help out with camp every day. In fact, he won't be here much at all. Even if he was, we'd still have a problem, because the park service expects us to have someone who's twenty-one here every day."

There were audible gasps as that bit of bad news sank in, but Leah's mind jumped straight to the next problem.

"Without you, who's going to drive the bus?" she asked Chris.

Chris just smiled and nodded across the circle.

"I am," David Altmann said with obvious satisfaction. "I can't think of anything I'd rather do this summer than hang out here with those kids."

Leah couldn't help noticing the way he looked at Caitlin when he said it, though, or the deep blush that colored Caitlin's cheeks in return.

"So David's going to be our camp director! Isn't that great?" Peter asked. "I know it's a load off my mind."

In that instant, Leah realized how concerned he must have been about the situation, yet he had never mentioned it to the group. It was just like him to worry in silence, to try to take care of things by himself.

*I wonder if he at least told Jenna.*

Leah glanced at her friend's face but found no answer there. She returned her gaze to Peter, only to catch him looking at Jenna too. Jenna's eyes met his, then quickly darted off. The smile died on his face.

*Poor Peter,* Leah thought. *For that matter, poor Jenna.*

Were they really going to break up? How would they ever get by without each other? Still . . .

*There's no way I'm stepping into that situation again.*
She had learned her lesson the first time.

# Eight

"I don't know why we have to go to church *today*," Dr. Jones griped from behind the wheel of his silver Mercedes.

"Because it's Easter," Elsa said calmly from the passenger seat. "I would have thought that was pretty clear."

"I *know* it's Easter. My gut's still reeling from that breakfast."

In the backseat, Jesse and Brittany stifled smiles. Elsa had gone all out for breakfast that morning, actually getting up early to fry the bacon herself. By the time Jesse had wandered downstairs, she had set out a huge feast on a dining room table decorated with flowers, candles, and chocolate eggs.

"You did all this yourself?" he had asked, astonished. There was sausage as well as bacon, three or four really fancy coffee cakes, a silver platter of scrambled eggs, and a crispy hash-brown casserole. Even the housekeeper didn't normally cook such fancy spreads, and she was off for the holiday.

"Sally put the casserole in the freezer before she

left on Friday," Elsa had admitted anxiously, smoothing her platinum hair into place. "The cakes are from La Petite Patisserie. But I did the rest."

"I'm impressed."

"Really?" She'd sounded nearly as surprised as Jesse was.

"Sure." He had walked slowly around the table. All the best china and silver were out, and the more he'd looked, the more things he had spotted lurking in the green plastic grass surrounding the long centerpiece: marshmallow chicks and jelly beans, foil-covered chocolate rabbits, and, at Brittany's place, a tiny porcelain basket with a pair of earrings in it.

"I just wanted it to be nice. For all of us, you know? And especially for Brittany. To help her . . . feel better about things."

Jesse had nodded as her meaning sank in. He wasn't the only one who had been walking on eggshells since Brittany's unexpected rebellion in January. Elsa seemed to be doing her best to repair the damage, although no one really wanted to talk about what had caused it.

"You know I hate big meals so early in the morning," Dr. Jones complained now as he drove. "After all that food, it'll be a miracle if I don't fall asleep in the pew."

"If it's a miracle, you'll be in the right place," Elsa said, prompting surprised snorts of laughter from the back.

Dr. Jones ignored the levity at his expense. "You know I don't like—"

"The food was there. No one made you overeat."

"No, but I . . . I . . ." Dr. Jones sputtered, unable to think of a comeback. "This is going to shoot half the day," he grumbled at last.

Elsa crossed her arms across the front of her new silk blouse. "I think it's nice that we're finally doing something together as a family. Maybe we ought to go to church every week."

Dr. Jones turned his head to search his wife's face. He didn't say anything, but Jesse caught his panicked expression. The threat of losing half a day of work *every* week had rendered him temporarily speechless. Elsa smiled and settled more comfortably into her seat, the expression on her face saying exactly what Jesse was thinking: She had finally won an argument.

Jesse looked over to find Brittany smiling at him again, her new earrings sparkling with the delighted bobbing of her head. He exchanged another secret grin with her, both of them laughing at his father.

And all of a sudden, he got an odd feeling. The adults debating in the front of the car, the kids conspiring in back . . . it almost felt like déjà vu. Jesse could remember days like this from back when his parents had been married. Back when his brothers had still been around.

Back when he'd had a family.

With a jolt he realized that was what was so odd. Elsa would never take his mother's place, and no one could consider a twelve-year-old girl a fair exchange for two older brothers. But something was happening just the same, something he'd never expected.

He, his father, Elsa, and Brittany: They *were* kind of like a family.


"Pretty cool baskets this year," Caitlin said, making Jenna jump. She hadn't heard her sister come in through their bedroom door.

"Yeah. They are."

The bulging Easter basket on her desk held a load of candy and chocolate, two CDs, a paperback, and a gold cross to replace the one she had given Sarah. The necklaces weren't identical, but her new one was just as pretty, and Jenna was looking forward to wearing it to church in a few minutes. Until Caitlin had walked in, however, Jenna had barely been aware of the basket in front of her. She'd been thinking of Peter and the Junior Explorers.

They'd be having an egg hunt at the park that morning, the way they had for the past two years. She'd helped out both times, and it had been fun watching the kids scurry around in search of eggs, squealing when they found one. This year, however, Peter hadn't invited her.

"I'm going down," Caitlin said, taking a coat from the closet. "We're almost ready to leave."

"Okay. I'll be there in a minute."

Caitlin nodded and left. Jenna sighed, her eyes still on the basket.

*He probably didn't think he needed to invite me. I could have just gone.*

But she hadn't, and now it was too late. The kids would be finishing up their cookies and juice in the activities center, showing off their best finds to their parents. In a few more minutes, they'd all be gone. *I have no one to blame for missing out but myself.*

After all, at the work party the day before, Peter had said he wanted to stay together, that he wanted to work things out. But once David had broken up their conversation, they had never found an opportunity to resume it. If anything, she had avoided talking to Peter, assigning herself tasks that kept her far away from him.

*It wasn't that I didn't want to talk to him. I just didn't want to talk to him there, about that. Not with all those people around every—*

"Jenna! Let's go, dear!" Mrs. Conrad's voice floated up the stairs.

In the garage, Jenna was the last to climb into her father's van. Sarah, Maggie, and Allison sat on the first bench, their frilly Easter dresses taking up more room than they did. Jenna dropped into the vacant space on the second bench beside Caitlin and Mary Beth, who had gotten home just an hour before. Her auburn curls looked tamer than when she'd arrived, but there were dark circles beneath her eyes that makeup couldn't erase, the result of cramming for midterms.

"This is a special day," Mrs. Conrad said, turning to smile at her daughters as the van backed onto the street. "All of us home again for the first time since the accident, going to church together . . . and on top of that it's Easter. I'll always remember Easter now as the week God gave us back Sarah. It seems appropriate, doesn't it?"

Sarah beamed. "This *is* a good Easter."

But Jenna's fingers crept to the new cross around her neck as she realized her mother's meaning. Jesus rose from the dead on Easter and, in a way, Sarah had risen too. Not that she'd actually died, but for a time it had seemed that she would, or at least that her brain would be so badly damaged that the Sarah they'd known would be gone. To have her back with them again, happy and whole, was nothing short of a second Easter miracle.

*I will not be unhappy*, Jenna vowed, staring at her sister with a renewed feeling of awe. *Not about Peter or anything else. Not on Easter. Not with Sarah safe.*

In the church parking lot, Mr. Conrad stopped at the curb to let everyone out before he parked. The five older girls piled out quickly, giving Mrs. Conrad room to help Sarah with her cane.

"We'll go right in," their mother said as the van drove away. "Sarah needs to sit down, and your dad knows where to find us."

"Good," said Mary Beth, yawning. "I need to sit down too."

They started toward the church door. All but Jenna. She hung back a moment, uncertain, and then she made up her mind.

"I'm going to wait out here and see Peter," she said.

Steadying Sarah with one arm, Mrs. Conrad glanced back over her shoulder. "All right, but don't be long. We need you in the choir."

"I'll be there," Jenna said, her eyes on the cars streaming into the lot.

Peter would be coming straight from the park, so he'd probably be driving his Toyota instead of riding with his parents. And, unless David had decided to tag along for the egg hunt, he'd probably be alone. It was a good chance to say something—anything— that might finish what they'd started the day before.

*I do not want to go back to school tomorrow with this thing still up in the air,* Jenna thought, growing more and more anxious as the minutes ticked by and the parking lot gradually filled. *I have to talk to him.*

At last she spotted the familiar blue Toyota pulling in to park. Peter was alone behind the wheel. Jenna was so relieved, she almost ran onto the pavement to greet him. Then, when he was halfway to the curb, she did.

"Hi," she said breathlessly. His hair was combed off his face, and the robin's-egg blue of his sweater brought out the blue of his eyes. His slacks were gray and immaculately pressed. He looked handsome, and sweet, and way too neat for someone who had spent the last two hours crawling around in the bushes. "Didn't you do the egg hunt?"

"Yeah, we did it. Why? Oh," he said, following the line of her gaze. "I changed clothes at the park."

She nodded, forcing herself to focus on the moment instead of the fun she'd missed. "You look nice."

"No, *you* look nice," Peter returned with a smile. "Except aren't you singing today? Where's your choir robe?"

Jenna glanced down at her watch. "Uh-oh. I've got to go get dressed. I just wanted . . . I wanted to say . . ."

She didn't know what she wanted to say.

"I'm busy with my family all day, and tonight we're going out to dinner, but meet me for lunch tomorrow," Peter urged.

Reaching for her hand, he began walking her toward the church. "Let's brown-bag it and eat somewhere quiet."

"All right," she agreed, feeling her hand melt into his. It had been so long since they had touched, she was barely aware of anything else—not the asphalt under her feet, not the gathering crowd of people in their Sunday best, not even the trouble she'd be in if she was late joining the choir. A lump formed in her throat as she matched her stride to his. Whatever had happened—or would happen—between them, he was still her best friend. Suddenly she wanted him to know how much she admired him, how much he inspired her . . . and how much she would always love him.

"Peter?"

"Yes?" The way he looked at her sent a jolt right through her heart.

"I . . . I . . . I'll meet you by your locker."

Miguel checked in early for his Sunday-afternoon shift at the hospital, wanting to spend a few extra minutes with Zach.

"Here comes the Easter bunny," he announced, walking through the boy's open door.

"You're the goofiest-looking Easter bunny I ever saw," Zach said.

"Hey! Don't insult the guy with the presents."

"Presents?" Zach sat up higher in bed. "What did you bring me?"

"Don't get *too* excited," Miguel warned. Producing his gift from behind his back, he watched Zach's eyes light up.

"Cool!"

"Now that's a *guy's* Easter basket," said Miguel, putting it into Zach's reaching hands. "Real men don't eat marshmallow chickens."

"Cool," Zach repeated, round-eyed. Instead of a

basket, Miguel had filled a Wildcats baseball hat with a chocolate rabbit surrounded by jelly beans and bubble gum.

"Where can I put the candy?" Zach asked.

Miguel laughed. "In your stomach."

"No, where can I put it *now?* I want to wear the hat."

"Oh. All right."

Looking around the room, Miguel found an unused plastic barf pan and held it out for Zach to dump his candy into. The moment the hat was empty, Zach put it on his head.

"How do I look?" he asked, craning his neck to give Miguel a good view. "Better with a hat on, right?"

Zach had never before mentioned the way his hair fell out in clumps from the chemotherapy, but it had thinned to the point that Miguel had guessed it might be starting to bother him.

"You look ready to hit a home run," said Miguel. "Here, let me see that a minute." Lifting the new green cap off Zach's head, he removed the tags and adjusted the strap to make it smaller. Then he put it back, tilting the bill up out of Zach's eyes.

"Hey, batter, batter," a female voice said behind them. Miguel turned to see Mrs. Dewey.

Compared to the last time he had seen her, in the ICU waiting room, she looked like the picture of health and relaxation. Her pale-pink sweats added softness to her thin frame, and her dark hair was tucked casually behind her ears. Her smile seemed easy, her laughter light. Only her eyes showed the strain of the past few weeks.

"Hi, Mrs. Dewey. I just brought Zach an Easter present. I hope that's all right," he added, belatedly realizing there wasn't any other candy in the room.

"It's fine. We don't normally celebrate Easter, but these are special circumstances."

Miguel's blank expression must have betrayed his confusion.

"We're Jewish," she explained.

"I—I'm sorry," he stammered, feeling like a fool. "I didn't even think—"

"It was *very* thoughtful. And I like that hat."

"It's cool, isn't it?" Zach asked, preening for her admiration.

"Did Zach tell you they've scheduled his surgery for next week?" Mrs. Dewey asked Miguel.

"No! That's fantastic!"

"I was just going to tell him," Zach said, frowning.

"But you have to be happy about that, bud! That means the tumor has shrunk. Once they get it out of there, you're halfway home."

Zach smiled wistfully at the mention of home, and Miguel suddenly wondered how much the boy knew about the surgery. To remove the cancerous kidney and the extensive tumor around it, the doctors were going to have to cut Zach open from above his heart down to his navel. If things went wrong, he could bleed to death, or his heart could stop—for good this time. Even thinking about it gave Miguel the shivers.

*The less he knows, the better,* Miguel decided. After all, there was no avoiding the surgery, and as scary as it was, Dr. Wells kept saying the vast majority of kids not only survived but recovered completely. *Why should Zach worry when he has so many people doing it for him?*

"It will be a big relief to have that behind us," Mrs. Dewey said as if reading his mind.

"Of course!" Miguel replied, trying to banish all traces of fear from his voice.

"It's probably going to be on Wednesday," Zach said. "Will you be here?"

"Are you kidding?" Miguel answered. "Try to keep me away."

A nurse passed by in the hall, then took a few steps backward to speak through the open door. "There you are, Miguel. Howard is looking for you."

"He is?" Miguel glanced at his watch and grimaced with the realization that he should have checked in fifteen minutes before. "Oops. I'll bet he is. I'll try to come back later, Zach. See you around, Mrs. Dewey."

"See you, Miguel," she said, smiling.

*I hope he's not mad,* Miguel thought as he slipped

out the door in search of Howard. *And I really hope he's not going to deliver another lecture about getting too attached to Zach.*

Not that it would do any good.

*That ship has already sailed anyway, and Howard probably knows it. It's way too late to warn me about that now. Besides, Mrs. Dewey doesn't seem to mind having me around. I bet she will let me hang out with Zach after he goes home. He ought to have some sort of guy in his life. I could be like a big brother to him.*

Miguel smiled as he hurried down the hallway.

*I'd like that. I'd like it a lot.*

# Nine

"Hey, Jenna! Need a ride home?" Leah called out her mother's car window on Monday. Miguel was going straight to the hospital that afternoon and the news had forecast rain, so her mother had let her drive.

Jenna turned her head and squinted against the bright sunshine. When she saw Leah, she ran across the street in front of CCHS, her hair flying out behind her.

"Thanks," she said, opening the passenger door. "I have a ton of books in my backpack today."

"Yeah. Me too." Leah pulled into traffic, then stopped at a light, taking the opportunity to study her friend more closely. "You're all dressed up today. Anything special going on?"

Jenna blushed and shook her head. "No, I just felt like wearing this. I don't get to very often."

"I didn't see you at lunch."

Jenna's blush deepened. "Peter and I ate on the soccer field bleachers."

"Really?" Leah asked hopefully. "Because on Saturday it seemed like—"

"I know, but Peter doesn't want to break up. We're going to try to work it out."

"That's great! I mean, you didn't want to break up either. Right?"

"I just thought . . . well . . . I felt like I ought to give *him* the chance."

"But if he didn't take it, what's left to work out? I don't see the problem."

The light changed, and Leah began driving again.

"Everything just feels weird now," Jenna said, staring out the window. "I mean, you and Miguel started out as boyfriend and girlfriend. With Peter and me it was different. It's strange enough going from being best friends with someone to being his girlfriend. But when you think that maybe he might have preferred someone else, that he just chose you because it was easy . . ."

Leah burst out laughing. "Sorry," she said, "but I don't think anyone could accuse you of making things easy."

Jenna gave a reluctant smile. "I guess not. It's just . . . at least when he didn't know I was upset with him about Melanie, I could pretend nothing was wrong. But now . . ." Jenna shrugged. "I know it's better to be honest and have everything out in the open. It just feels kind of worse."

Leah cringed, knowing whose fault that was. "I'm really sorry, Jenna. I'm so mad at myself for—"

"That's okay."

They drove awhile in silence, out of things to say. Leah wanted to encourage Jenna to stick things out with Peter, but how could she without butting in again?

"Are you guys going to the prom?" she asked as they turned the last corner before Jenna's house. "It's not that far off. You might as well start planning now."

"Are you and Miguel going to the prom?"

"Of course."

Although now that Leah stopped to think about it, he hadn't asked her yet. *On the other hand, he'd be dead if he asked anyone else. And it is senior year. Of course we're going.*

"Well, Peter hasn't mentioned it. But if he asks me . . ." Jenna sighed. "He took Melanie to the homecoming dance."

"Jenna, you have to let this go," Leah said impatiently. "I'm telling you the truth."

"I know."

"If he asks you and you say no, then what? Do you want him to go with somebody else?"

"No, I'll go," Jenna said quickly. "I just wish . . . I wish . . ."

"What?"

"I wish Melanie had a boyfriend."

* * *

"All right. That's all for today," Sandra called over the din in the gym on Tuesday. She blew her whistle a couple of times to get her point across, and gradually the mob of cheerleading hopefuls grew quiet.

"We have one more practice on Friday, then first-cut tryouts next Wednesday. I would suggest you all practice on your own this week, so if you find any rough spots, you can get help Friday. Questions? Good. See you then."

A nervous rumble ran through the dispersing crowd, and Melanie remembered the fear she'd felt trying out the year before. In a way, she felt sorry for the candidates. They would all be nervous wrecks for the next week; then only four would make it.

*Will one of those four be Nicole?* she wondered, trying to spot her in the chaos.

Melanie had convinced Nicole to join Vanessa's group that day, and they'd been working out on the other side of the gym.

"You already know everything I know," Melanie had rationalized, "and it's better if we don't look too buddy-buddy. Besides, Vanessa may be an amateur human being, but she's a good cheerleader. You could pick up some useful tips."

To her surprise, Nicole hadn't argued. Instead, she'd trotted off and joined Vanessa's group, radiating confidence. She seemed almost a different girl now from the klutz who had bumbled through the first practice.

*Thanks to me*, Melanie thought with a certain satisfaction. *She couldn't cheer her way out of a paper bag before I started coaching her. Now—*

"Good practice today," Sandra said at her side.

Melanie jerked her head around, startled back to the present. "Yeah. I think we have some good prospects."

"You have your eye on anyone in particular?" Sandra asked casually.

Melanie's heart sped up. Was her coach hinting at something?

"No. Well. I mean, a lot of the girls are good. There are probably twenty who could fill a spot, and ten who are downright awesome. If we wanted to, we could have the biggest squad in Missouri."

"I see great minds think alike," Sandra said with a cryptic smile. "After all, there's nothing magic about eight, is there?"

"N-No," Melanie answered, heart pounding. Was Sandra saying what it sounded like? Was she going to open more spots?

"You probably think I've gone over the top with all these practices, but cheerleading is more than dancing and memorizing yells. If you're not dedicated to being a team, you'll never be any good. Between us, I felt like we had some dedication problems this year.

I want to make sure that next year's squad is ready to work."

"And so you've been watching people's attendance," Melanie guessed.

Sandra smiled. "Like a hawk. And I've been watching how they take direction, and how they work with others. I agree: We have a lot of solid candidates. It would be hard to pick just four."

Melanie glanced around the gym. A lot of people were still hanging out, changing their shoes or talking to friends, but no one was listening to her and Sandra. "And so you're saying . . . ?"

"I'm not saying anything officially, so don't you dare repeat this. I just think we have the depth of field to consider a bigger squad." Sandra winked, a conspirator's gesture. "I'm *considering*, that's all."

"I see," Melanie said, trying to hide her excitement. Even a couple more spots would give Nicole a much better chance.

"Not a word, though," Sandra repeated before she walked off. "I still haven't made up my mind."

Nicole was waiting by Melanie's gym bag on the bleachers. "What were you and Sandra talking about?" she asked the moment Melanie got there.

"Nothing. This and that." Melanie unzipped her bag and took out a hairbrush.

"Mela-*nie*," Nicole whined.

"I can't tell you. She told me not to."

"Was it about me?" Nicole whispered, wide-eyed.

"What? Of course not."

Nicole looked as if her every hope had been dashed. She was so transparent it was actually funny sometimes.

*If she only knew what Sandra's considering, she'd be bouncing off the walls.*

*Which is just another reason not to tell her.*

Even so, Melanie couldn't resist a hint. "Look, I can't say what we were talking about, because Sandra would be mad. But let's just say that your odds of making the squad might have gotten a little better."

Nicole looked as if she were going to swoon. "That's the best news *ever*," she gushed, collapsing on the bottom bleacher. "Oh, I hope. I hope, I hope." Squeezing her eyes shut, she crossed fingers on each hand, then crossed her thumbs as well. "It's all I really want."

"Then you don't want much." Melanie tossed her hairbrush in on top of her shoes and towel and zipped her gym bag closed.

"What?"

"Never mind. I'm ready to go. Are you?"

They walked out of the gym, Melanie shivering in the afternoon shadows. Compared to the overheated atmosphere indoors, the outside air was freezing. She was rubbing down the goose bumps on her arms, wishing she'd worn long sleeves, when a movement out of the corner of her eye made her forget all about being cold.

"I just remembered something. I'll meet you at the car," she said, shoving her gym bag into Nicole's arms. Before Nicole could protest, Melanie took off running.

"Steve!" she called, jogging up the rise to the access road through school. She could only see the top of a white-blond head, but she was positive it belonged to Steve Carson, the not-unappealing guy who sat in the front of her art history class. She had never spoken to him before, but now seemed like the perfect time to start. "Steve, wait up!"

Steve turned, then stood waiting for her to close the distance between them. He was obviously astonished, but she gave him points for trying to hide it.

"Hi, Melanie. What's going on?" he asked.

She smiled. More points for not pretending he didn't know who she was. She'd seen him checking her out in art class, although he probably didn't realize that. Guys always thought they were so sly.

"Hi, Steve." She hesitated a moment, pretending she needed to catch her breath. Steve was over six feet tall, with high, wide cheekbones and a squared-off jaw. His hair was so pale he might have seemed washed out if not for his piercing blue eyes. "I was just wondering if you remember what the homework assignment was today. I thought I wrote it down, but . . . was it chapter eight or chapter nine?"

She smiled as if unaware that she'd just used the

most transparent excuse in history. It was *supposed* to be transparent. That was part of her plan.

"Um, it was chapters eight *and* nine."

Melanie sighed even though she had already read the entire book for fun. "How are you doing in that class? It's a lot of work, isn't it?"

"It is," he said slowly, "but I like it. Painting is kind of a hobby of mine."

"Really? Mine too!"

More points for Steve. Plus, his looks were definitely starting to grow on her. He had nice teeth, she decided, and she really liked his thick, straight hair. Broad through the chest, narrow through the hips . . . *He'll look great in a tuxedo.*

"Well, thanks for the help," she said, flashing him her sweetest, most flirtatious smile. "See you in class tomorrow."

She turned and sauntered off, slowly enough to give him the benefit of the view.

"Yeah . . . uh . . . tomorrow," he called after her, finding his voice a few seconds too late.

Melanie grinned to herself.

*Let the games begin.*

# Ten

"I really think I have a chance to make the squad this year," Nicole told Courtney, jabbing her finger in the air for emphasis. "I mean it. Really."

"Uh-huh."

The way Courtney was gazing off across the cafeteria, Nicole knew her friend wasn't listening, but it was hard to stop talking when she was so excited.

"I wouldn't say so if it was only wishful thinking." Lowering her voice to a whisper, Nicole imparted the most thrilling news of all. "You can't say *anything* to *anyone*, but Melanie's being really encouraging. I think *she* thinks I'll get on."

"That's good," Courtney said blandly.

"I'm glad you're so happy for me," Nicole retorted sarcastically.

"Uh-huh. I am."

*I give up. She's hopeless*, thought Nicole, sitting back in disgust. Courtney was sure to be looking for Kyle, who had yet to show up that Wednesday.

*Unless she's looking for Emily Dooley.*

Nicole glanced around, trying to locate Courtney's old junior-high friend. Not long ago, Emily had actually seemed like a threat to Nicole's friendship with Courtney. Lately, though, Courtney seemed to have forgotten all about her, and Emily had drifted back to her other friends.

*There she is*, Nicole thought, spotting Emily at her usual table. *I guess I should be glad of that, at least.*

"Well, look who's finally here," Courtney said under her breath.

Nicole's eyes left Emily to follow Courtney's gaze to the main door. Kyle had just walked in, looking like he was posing for somebody's camera.

"Gotta go," Courtney said.

"Courtney! You can't just leave me here."

"Okay, see you later." Slinging her backpack over one shoulder, Courtney took off without a backward glance.

She strode through the first few tables, and then she started to trot. Kyle turned, caught sight of her, and flashed his best babe-magnet grin. Running the last few feet, Courtney actually jumped into his arms, as if she had read the same cheesy script he seemed to be working by. The whole thing was so obviously fake it made Nicole want to vomit.

*Maybe if Jeff had been nicer to her on Saturday . . .*

Courtney was never going to admit it, but Nicole was pretty sure she was getting fed up with Kyle and his fooling around. As long as no one else at school knew about it, though, and as long as Jeff kept

115

ignoring her, she would carry on the charade, too stubborn to give up.

*He didn't have to be that cold.*

Granted, Jeff had been there with his new girlfriend, and Courtney shouldn't have been there at all, but he had treated her as if she were invisible.

Which was actually kind, considering what an idiot she was being. He had to have noticed. But somehow he had managed to give the illusion of being so into Hope he didn't see anyone else.

Not that Nicole thought he *wasn't* into Hope.

*That's the whole problem.*

She made no effort to pretend she wasn't staring as Kyle swung Courtney around like an actor in a phony mouthwash commercial.

*What does* he *get out of this?* Nicole wondered. *I mean, at least Court's making a fool of herself for a reason. But Kyle—*

"A person could lose his lunch," a voice said at Nicole's side. Startled, she turned to see Jeff standing there, a completely disgusted look on his face.

"What?" she asked, trying to sound innocent. But it was no use. She could feel the blush burning up her cheeks.

"*The Kyle and Courtney Show.* If you're really her friend, you ought to talk some sense into her."

"I don't know what—"

"I'll tell you the truth," he said, still staring at Courtney. "At first I felt kind of sorry for her, but now

I'm embarrassed we ever dated. She's making us *all* look bad."

*I know*, Nicole groaned to herself as he stalked away.

If she hadn't been self-conscious enough before, now it seemed every eye in the cafeteria was turning from Courtney to her. All but Courtney's, of course. Her face was still glued to Kyle's.

*At least she didn't see me talking to Jeff. If she had, she'd have demanded to know what he said.*

Nicole shook her head. No matter how big a fool Courtney made of herself, that was one message she would never pass along.

*I couldn't. Court would be absolutely destroyed.*

Miguel was the first one standing at the end of sixth period. His teacher was still talking over the bell, trying to finish a point, but Miguel was out the door before most of his classmates had even zipped their packs.

The entire day had been torture. He'd been worried since the moment he'd woken up, and only the knowledge that Zach wouldn't be out of surgery until two-thirty had kept him from ditching lunch and going straight to the hospital. Now he sprinted down the main hallway, trying to get out of the building before the passage became choked with students.

In the parking lot, Miguel tried to start his car, buckle his seat belt, and back out all at the same time. He wanted to be good and gone before the usual traffic jam. Safely on the street at last, he breathed a sigh of relief. He was finally on his way.

*You need to calm down*, he told himself, taking a few deep breaths. *It's not going to reassure anyone if you show up in a panic. You shouldn't even be in a panic. Everything's going to be fine.*

So why did he keep imagining the worst possible outcomes? Ever since Zach's surgery had begun that morning, Miguel had been telling himself horror stories about everything that could go wrong: The tumor had ruptured during removal, spreading cancer cells throughout Zach's body; cancer had been discovered in *both* kidneys; Dr. Wells hadn't been able to get all of the tumor out; Zach had bled to death; his heart had seized on the table . . .

"Stop it!" Miguel ordered himself. "You're being ridiculous."

By the time he'd parked in the hospital lot and run into the lobby, he felt light-headed. His hand shook as he raised a finger to press the elevator button. Because the surgery was so major, Zach would be going into intensive care immediately afterward. The elevator doors opened on the ICU waiting room and Miguel sucked in his breath.

*This is it*, he thought, stepping onto the floor. The clock over the nurses' station read nearly three. In a moment he'd know the news he'd been waiting for all day—and it was almost certainly going to be better than he feared. *After all*, he reminded himself, *the majority of kids survive this*.

He was rushing forward when Mrs. Dewey emerged from the hall to the bathrooms.

"Mrs. Dewey! What are you doing here?" he exclaimed. "I thought you'd be in there with Zach."

"Zach's still in surgery," she said, checking her watch.

"*Still?*" His voice sounded loud and frightened in the silent room. "I mean, not that there's anything *wrong*," he added quickly. "It's just . . . they're probably finishing up right now."

"Probably." Mrs. Dewey looked at her watch again. Her eyes were bloodshot, he noticed, and there were permanent worry lines between her brows.

"I'll wait with you," Miguel offered. "Did they tell Zach I called this morning?"

Mrs. Dewey nodded as they took a couple of seats. "Dr. Wells told him you'd be here when he woke up. Zach knows he won't be able to see you right away, but it made him feel better to know you'd be around. He really likes you, Miguel."

"I like him." But the catch in his voice was so obvious that Miguel didn't trust himself to say more. Instead he stared straight ahead, pretending a sudden interest in the opposite wall. It took all the self-control he had to wipe the emotion from his face.

*Mrs. Dewey has to be twice as scared as you are. To show your fear here is just plain selfish.*

He concentrated on making his breathing even, his expression confident—but inside he was going crazy.

*It's been too long. Something has to be wrong.*

The minutes ticked by on the big wall clock, each one lasting an hour. Miguel didn't speak. Mrs. Dewey didn't speak. By three-thirty they weren't even looking at each other, afraid of what they'd read in each other's faces.

*Someone should have come out here by now. Someone should have told us something.*

If he only knew more people in the hospital, maybe he could make someone get them an update. In the anguish of the moment, it seemed that any news at all would be better than the limbo he was in. He was on the verge of running off to find Howard when Dr. Wells walked into the waiting room. One look at his face, and Miguel almost passed out.

From relief.

"We got it all," the doctor said happily. "Every bit of it. It took longer than I expected, but things couldn't have gone better. We removed those metastases from the lungs and sampled a few lymph nodes. Everything else looked clean. The liver was clean, the other kidney was fine. He'll spend a couple of days in the ICU, but that's just a precaution. He came through with flying colors."

"Thank you," Mrs. Dewey said calmly. And then she burst into tears.

"I'm just so relieved," she explained between sobs, taking the tissue the doctor offered. "I know it's silly to cry now."

"I see it all the time," Dr. Wells reassured her. "It's a completely normal reaction." Glancing at Miguel, he must have noticed a second set of wet cheeks. "*Completely* normal," he repeated with a smile.

"I . . . I have to . . . Tell Zach I said hi," Miguel got out before he hurried off, not wanting to shed more tears in public.

*Zach's fine. He's* better *than fine*, he thought happily, punching the button for the top floor. He could feel his heart rising up in his chest, keeping pace with the elevator. The heavy door slid open and Miguel stepped out, wiping his eyes on his sleeve. He felt set free, as light as oil on water. He wanted to skip in the empty corridor, to dance down the hall. No one was there to see him, and he was suddenly brimming with the strangest energy, the purest imaginable joy. He took a few reckless twirls, arms open wide, before an open doorway caught his attention, stopping him in his tracks.

He had found the hospital chapel.

"Perfect." He wanted to light a candle, to say a

prayer of thanks. He ducked inside to find he was the only person there.

There was no cross, no bank of burning candles—the room seemed meant to serve all faiths. But there were still padded benches, and flowers, and light streaming through colored windows. And there was a sense of something big there, much bigger than he. Dropping to his knees, Miguel simply opened his heart and let his thanks float heavenward. He had no words for the gratitude he felt. He didn't need them, anyway.

*Maybe I'll be a pediatric surgeon too. Just like Dr. Wells. What an awesome gift you gave him, God. And how much more awesome still to share it with someone like Zach. If you think I'm up for it . . . if you think I could . . . I'd work so hard for a gift like that.*

# *Eleven*

Melanie stood at the edge of the cafeteria, lunch tray in hand, waiting to make her move. There was a lot of delicate timing involved with this sort of thing. Besides, lately lunchtime was her only Jesse sighting all day, and she wanted to make the moment last.

*There he is*, she thought, her heart tugging toward him. He was sitting with the football players, his profile turned her way, his brown hair falling forward as he spoke to a friend across the table. Her hands clenched her tray with the desire to bury her fingers in those locks, to push them back off his face, to trace the perfect line of his lips. . . .

*Okay. Enough. Why torture yourself?*

Tearing her gaze from Jesse, she searched for Steve Carson's blond head instead, smiling when she spotted him in a brand-new location—one suspiciously close to the cheerleaders' table. Obviously the last two days of flirting had made the right impression. With a final glance down at the clingy new dress she was wearing, Melanie began her walk.

There was an art to crossing a crowded cafeteria. A person had to take her time, had to seem all but unaware of her surroundings while still giving the impression that she knew exactly where she was going. Most important of all was appearing completely oblivious to the heads turning one's way—that was the key to turning them in the first place. When most of the cafeteria was looking, when all the right eyes were on her, Melanie slowed down, milking the last few moments. She had done it a hundred times, but there was more than usual riding on her performance that day.

*Nice and slow,* she reminded herself as she headed toward the cheerleaders' table. *No need to hurry.*

If she wanted to be sure of a good prom date, it couldn't hurt to remind people that she was available. She was nearly at her seat, sauntering the last twenty feet, when something unexpected happened.

Jesse called out her name.

"Melanie! Hey, come here a minute."

She glanced back over her shoulder, her eyes meeting his with a jolt. "Be right there," she said, trying not to show her surprise. What could Jesse want?

She forced herself to walk the rest of the way to her table, dropping her tray off next to Tanya before slowly returning to see. "What's up?" she asked from across his table, where she could look him in the face.

"Nothing. I was just . . . um . . ."

He was completely surrounded by Wildcats. Suddenly it seemed that every one of them had stopped talking to listen to their conversation. Melanie smiled weakly, wishing too late that she had walked around to Jesse's side of the table.

"Yes?"

"I just . . . is there an Eight Prime meeting tonight?"

"What? No."

He'd called her over for that? She felt incredibly let down, and she wasn't even sure why. It wasn't as if she had expected *him* to ask her out. But since she was already there . . .

"So," she said flirtatiously, leaning forward enough to make eye contact with both sides of the table. "Do you guys all have prom dates yet?"

She smiled around at the group: Gary Baldwin, Barry Stein, Nate Kilriley—they weren't her type. But maybe Josh Stockton. Or better still, Hank Lundgreen.

"You've got to be kidding," said Josh. "The prom is still over two weeks away. It's too early to worry about dates."

"That's right," said Barry, to general nods. If any of them had made their selection, no one wanted to admit it.

"The good ones go early," Melanie countered, tossing her hair. She hesitated just long enough to let her words sink in before she turned and walked away.

She never looked behind her, but she heard the muted ruckus as she sat down next to Tanya. She could imagine what they were saying. And part of her couldn't help hoping that Jesse was eating his heart out.

"What was that about?" Tanya asked curiously.

"Nothing. Just making a little point."

"And did they get it?"

Melanie nodded. "Definitely."

If she didn't have the prom sewn up in the next few days, she'd be amazed.

"So what should we do this weekend?" Peter asked, leaning against the locker next to Jenna's. Classes were out for the day, and the hall had emptied enough for a private conversation. "Do you want to go out Friday night?"

"You mean, like, on a date?" she asked hesitantly.

"Okay." He smiled as if she'd been the one to suggest it.

Jenna turned to rummage in her locker, not knowing what to say. For the last four days she and Peter had been hanging out together at school, but something still didn't feel right. She'd tried hard to forget, to put the past behind them, but once doubts had entered a relationship, could it ever be the same? Was it really possible to go back to the way things had been before? Jenna wasn't mad anymore; she wasn't even upset. All she felt was a deep, aching sadness for the way things might have been.

"I don't think I can," she said at last. "We keep pushing this, Peter, but we aren't getting anywhere."

The smile died on Peter's face. "What do you mean, we aren't getting anywhere? Where do you want to go?"

"I mean it's not the same." She could feel herself getting choked up, but she forced the words past the lump in her throat. "I know this is all my fault. There are so many things I should have done differently. But what happened, happened. And I feel like the more we try to deny it, the less chance we have of salvaging anything out of this. I can take not being your girlfriend, but I can't take not being your friend."

She thought she had finally put her case pretty well. Maybe the time they'd been spending together had helped her find the right words. But Peter shook his head.

"Jenna, you're *more* than my friend. I love you."

"I love you, too, but—"

"No buts! Do you love me or not?"

"You know I do."

"Not really. Not anymore. Maybe if you ever let it show . . ."

Jenna closed her eyes. She didn't know what he wanted. All she knew was that a nighttime date was too much pressure, and she was already cracking under the strain.

"I just . . . maybe we can do something during the weekend. Mary Beth is leaving Saturday, so I should probably hang around for her last day. But what about Sunday, after church?"

"*Right* after church," Peter agreed immediately. "Save your afternoon."

"All right, but I have to go now. I'm meeting Jenny Brown in the library."

"Oh, yeah. That civics paper, right?"

"Right. I'll see you later."

She escaped down the hallway, more confused than she'd ever been. Peter was doing everything right, was saying all the right things. And she *did* love him. So why couldn't she show it? And why should she have to worry about showing it at all? Shouldn't it show itself?

*This is making me crazy*, she thought, a lone tear slipping down her cheek. *If everything's supposed to be fixed now, then why does it still feel broken?*

"Ha! I got you!" Miguel crowed, running up the Astroturf to join Leah. The hole they were playing was shaped like a miniature volcano, with lurid red and orange paint running down its sides. In the darkness of early evening, with a black light shining on it, it almost seemed to glow.

"Aren't you proud of yourself?" Leah returned with a laugh, watching their balls roll into the curb.

"You do know this is golf and not croquet? You don't get any points for hitting my ball."

"It's all part of my secret plan," Miguel said, waggling his brows.

Leah laughed again, not even minding that it took her six strokes to knock her ball up the volcano's steep slopes and into its central cup.

"You're in a good mood tonight," she said, leaning on her putter while Miguel whacked away with his, trying to duplicate her feat. "Are you happy because it's Friday, or is it just the thrill of my company?"

"Oh, it's you. Of *course*," he said, trying to scoot his ball up on the side of his club instead of actually hitting it.

"You're just saying that so I won't call you on your cheating."

"Am I cheating?" he asked with astonished innocence.

"Not much." Leah turned her head long enough to let him put the ball in by hand.

"Will you look at that?" he exclaimed, pointing triumphantly. "Oh, no. You missed my shot!"

"Imagine," she said with a playful roll of her eyes. Resting her club on her shoulder, she started walking to the next hole. She couldn't care less if Miguel wanted to take a few shortcuts. They weren't keeping score anyway, so why not have a good time? The source of Miguel's high spirits was no mystery either, despite her earlier teasing. They were there to celebrate Zach's recovery.

Putting her ball on the tee, she waited to time the rotation on the blades of the blue-and-white windmill, then swung as hard as she could. The ball zipped up the long ramp over the water, went cleanly between whirling blades, and rolled down toward the easy hole on the other side.

"Yes!" she cried, jumping up and down. "Let's see you top that, Miguel! Oh, and by the way, that ramp won't hold your weight."

"You think I would climb out there? I'm hurt."

"You look hurt."

"Why don't you kiss me and make it better?"

The miniature golf course was far from deserted, but there wasn't a crowd right around them. Each hole was a little oasis of bright lights surrounded by darkness. Leah barely hesitated before she gave him what he had asked for, dancing away before he could grab her for more.

"I don't know what came over me," she teased, giggling. "It must be this ultraromantic place you've taken me to."

"It *is* romantic. Look, it's got a waterfall," he said, pointing hopefully at a trickle under the windmill.

"It's practically Hawaii."

Miguel hit his ball, miraculously managing to duplicate her shot. "Now I think we need to walk down this dark path, through all these tall bushes . . ."

"You sweet-talker, you."

Leah skipped ahead of him, but he caught her at the narrowest part of the path. Holding her tightly, he lowered his lips to hers, plying her with soft, teasing kisses, until she kissed him back. Minutes later, when he let her go, her knees almost buckled beneath her.

"I told you this is romantic," he said smugly. "It's the waterfall."

"That's some waterfall. Maybe we should come back here after prom."

It was a major hint, but the moment was so right she couldn't resist. *I just want to hear him say we're going.* Especially since she planned to buy something really spectacular to wear.

"You want to come here? Because I was thinking I could do a little better."

"Really? What did you have in mind?"

"Maybe I want to surprise you," he said mysteriously.

Leah smiled, wondering what he was planning. "You have to give me some idea, though, so I know how to dress. I mean, are we going to be indoors, outdoors, or what?"

"Not telling," said Miguel, "but that backless number you wore to homecoming looked pretty good to me."

"That's easy for you to say. You're not the one who's going to freeze."

"You won't freeze," he promised, grinning. "I know how to keep you warm."

131

Leah made a face. "And you're so modest about it too."

"I try." Putting an arm around her, he started up the path toward their balls, but she dragged her feet, not satisfied.

"We're definitely going, then?" she asked.

"Going where?"

"To the prom."

"Of course." A shadow crossed his face. "What's the matter? Don't you want to?"

"Of course I want to!"

He smiled again and began pushing her along. "Then watch out, Cinderella, because Price Charming will be on his game that night."

# Twelve

"I thought you knew how to do this." Laughing, Guy grappled with Nicole's elbow, trying to keep her on her feet.

"I never said that," Nicole replied testily, scrabbling to get her balance on the slippery ice. Her rented skates gave her no support, and every time she got a blade beneath her, her ankle gave out. "Just get me to the rail," she demanded, gazing longingly at the handhold a few unattainable feet away.

"What do you think I'm *trying* to do? A throw double axel?"

"I don't even know what you're talking about," she whimpered.

At last he got her to the boards, where she held on for dear life. Guy leaned against the rail beside her.

"Not bad," he said with a chuckle. "We've been on the ice five whole minutes."

"I'm just catching my breath," Nicole said testily, wondering how long she had to fake it before she could quit with dignity. After all, ice-skating had been her idea, and Guy had driven them all the way to Cave Creek to do it. "I think there's something wrong with these skates."

"You can always exchange them for another pair."

"I might. In a minute."

*Why does this look so easy on TV?* she wondered unhappily. At least she knew better now than to let go of the rail. As long as she kept a grip on that, she could pull herself back to the opening she'd stepped through to get to the ice. The concrete floor on the other side was covered with rubber padding, which wasn't *easy* to walk on, but at least that was possible.

"You're no Tara Lipinski, but you're still kind of cute," Guy said, looking her over. "When your cheeks turn pink like that, your eyes seem twice as blue."

"Oh. W-Well," Nicole stammered, feeling her cheeks grow even pinker at the unexpected compliment. "Thank you."

"I feel like having hot chocolate. Do you? I'm buying."

"Well, okay," she said, trying not to sound as thrilled as she actually was to get off the ice. "We have plenty of time to skate."

Keeping a death grip on the boards, she dragged herself back to the gate against the flow of traffic, ignoring the dirty looks from the other skaters. Guy took her elbow again, steadying her as they made their way to the nearest bench. He was so sturdy on his feet that she was starting to suspect he knew what he was doing, but she'd turned out to be so lame she didn't want to ask.

"Why don't you wait here and I'll go get the drinks?"

"Make mine tea, not chocolate," Nicole called after him, thinking of the new green shorts she was saving for cheerleading tryouts. There wasn't any room for a blob of whipped cream in those.

He was back in a few minutes, a steaming Styrofoam cup in each hand. "I forgot the sugar for your tea," he said, trying to hand both cups to her. "I'll have to go back and get it."

"No, plain is better. I, uh, I have something big coming up next week," she added, in response to his suspicious look. Heather had told him—and everyone else in their vacation Bible class—that Nicole had some sort of eating disorder.

"Yeah? What?" he asked, sitting on the bench beside her.

"It's just, uh . . . a thing," she faltered.

When she had called Guy that Saturday morning and asked him to go skating, she had meant to find out once and for all whether she liked him. For a while she had been sure she did. Then, after that fiasco in the bowling alley, she had been pretty sure she didn't. Seeing him and Jenna together at the Junior Explorers work party, though, had made her start thinking that maybe she did again. With everything else going on in her life, she would have liked to postpone worrying about Guy for a while, but with the prom coming up so soon, he was something she definitely needed to figure out. After all, she'd need a date—and if she and Guy were dating, it probably ought to be him.

Her plan that day had involved being nice to him and seeing how nice he could be in return. And even though she'd hit an unanticipated snag with the skating, he'd passed her test so far. If all went well for the entire date, she would ask him to the CCHS prom. Maybe he'd ask her to his, too, if they had one at his school. But if he upset her again . . .

"Oh, a *thing*," he said wryly. Her explanation hadn't flown.

*Just go ahead and tell him.* She had to admit she kind of wanted to anyway. Cheerleading had become practically all she could think about, and now that she had such a good chance of making the squad, she felt more inclined to let him in on her secret than she had when she'd first started practicing.

"I'm auditioning for something."

Guy's eyes widened with interest. "You mean, like a play? I didn't know you could act."

"Not a play." Nicole took a deep breath and flashed him the game-day smile she'd been practicing for two weeks. "I'm going out for the cheerleading squad. It looks like I'm going to make it too."

"Oh." Only one word, but there was no mistaking

the disapproval behind it. "I thought you were done with that sort of thing."

"What sort of thing?" she asked defensively.

"Nothing. It's just that cheerleading is kind of . . . lame. And shallow."

"Shallow?" she repeated, furious. "I didn't know you were such a cheerleading expert."

"What's to know? It's just posing, isn't it? After you gave up on modeling, I kind of thought—"

"It isn't posing! For your information, cheerleading's hard. I shouldn't even be here today. I *ought* to be home practicing. If it wasn't for—"

She cut herself off abruptly. There was no way she wanted to tell him why they were there now. Not after he'd just called her a poser.

"For what?" he asked.

"Nothing," she said sullenly, pretending to watch the skaters.

"Look, I'm sorry if—"

"Just forget about it."

*She* certainly had. She'd stay home before she asked him anywhere after the way he'd just insulted her.

*Besides, not everyone shares Guy's low opinion of cheerleading. If I make the squad, all kinds of guys will want to take me to the prom. Cute guys. From my own school.*

Nicole smiled at the thought. Things were finally

about to change for her. Next year she had the chance to actually *be* someone. Someone popular.

*Oh, well. His loss.*

"Zach! You're here! How are you feeling?" Miguel asked excitedly, finding the boy back on the children's ward Saturday.

Zach barely opened his eyes. "Like a car ran over me."

"Don't joke about that," Miguel said, superstitiously knocking on Zach's bedside tray. "I know someone that happened to."

Zach managed a weak smile, as if not really sure Miguel wasn't joking.

"I brought a new book," said Miguel, taking a seat by the bed. "Do you want me to read it to you?"

"No, I like the other one," Zach said groggily.

"Me too. But we finished it. Remember?"

"Oh, yeah." Zach seemed barely able to stay awake. *He's still recovering from the surgery*, thought Miguel. Dr. Wells probably had him on pain medication, not to mention the ongoing chemo and the radiation he'd be getting now. *No wonder he's tired. Poor kid.*

"I was here when you had your surgery. Did your mom tell you?"

"Yeah, but I don't remember anything because I was asleep. They cut me wide open." Zach pointed to the bandage around his torso.

138

"I know. And you did really well. Dr. Wells told me he got the whole tumor out."

Zach smiled dreamily. "That's what he told me, too. That's good, isn't it?"

"It's great! You ought to have smooth sailing from here on out."

Zach's smile grew wider even as his eyes dropped closed. A moment later the rhythm of his breathing indicated he had fallen asleep. Miguel looked down at the book he'd brought, a mystery involving a spooky old house, then set it on the bedside tray. Maybe after his nap Zach would want to start it himself.

Miguel was about to slip out when Dr. Wells appeared in the doorway.

"How's he doing?" the doctor asked.

"He just fell asleep," Miguel whispered back. "He seems pretty happy, but he can't keep his eyes open."

Dr. Wells nodded and motioned Miguel to join him in the hall. "Let him sleep, then. I was going to check his incision, but I can come back at the end of my rounds."

"I still can't believe what a miracle this is," Miguel said. "I mean, not that I didn't trust you, but when you came into that waiting room and said you'd gotten the cancer all out, it was like, like . . . I don't know. Something fantastic."

"It was a very successful surgery."

But there was a trace of something in Dr. Wells's

expression that hadn't been there on Wednesday. Miguel felt his stomach clench. It looked a lot like doubt.

"So everything's going to be fine. Right?" Miguel prompted.

Dr. Wells nodded. "Probably," he said, scratching his neck. "I'm still quite hopeful. But we did get some bad news back from the lab."

"What?"

"Until we took it out on Wednesday, we thought the tumor had a favorable histology. That would be the 'good' kind of cancer, the type with the highest cure rate."

Miguel nodded impatiently. He already knew that.

"Well, the lab's had a look at it now and it's anaplastic. That changes things some. The statistics aren't as good for anaplastic tumors."

"But if you got it all out, what difference does it make?"

"The cancer's more likely to come back with this type of tumor, and Zach's already had spots on his lungs." Dr. Wells shook his head. "On the bright side, though, the lymph nodes we sampled were negative."

"Negative's good?"

"In this case, yes," Dr. Wells said with a smile. "I'd still say Zach's chances are very good. I just wish . . . well. We work with the cards we're dealt."

"Right," said Miguel, determined to focus on the

positive. "And so far things have gone perfectly, right? I mean, everything except this histology part."

"I suppose you could say that. If perfect is relative."

"He's going to beat this. I know it," Miguel said with conviction. "He's going to get well, and grow up, and have a normal life. There's no way he's made it this far for no reason."

"That's the spirit," said Dr. Wells. "Zach's really lucky to have you around."

"I'm lucky to have him. Meeting Zach, seeing what he's been through, has inspired me more than ever to go to medical school."

"Did you get that application turned in yet?"

"Yep. Clearwater University."

"You'll get in."

"I know."

Miguel's smile was cocky as Dr. Wells waved and walked off down the hall. He couldn't have said why, but he had never been more confident about things in his life. Something had changed on Wednesday, when he had learned that Zach had come through the surgery so well. He was convinced now that there were bigger forces at work, strings being pulled by an unseen hand.

*I'll get into CU,* he thought, *and Zach will get out of here.* He was so positive, he felt almost giddy.

*Dr. Wells and I brought Zach this far, we'll take him the rest of the way.*

\* \* \*

141

"Oh, here's a good one!" Brittany said, using her finger to mark the place she was reading. " 'How Do You Know if He Likes You?' "

"If *who* likes you?" Jesse asked irritably. All he really wanted to do was wash his car in peace, but for the last half hour Brittany had been hanging around reading from some stupid girls' magazine. The weather was clear that Saturday, the Joneses' wide front lawn the bright green color of spring, and the driveway was actually warm beneath his bare feet. It was the perfect day to put a couple of CDs in the changer and detail his car, polishing it till it shone. Instead, Brittany had turned his music down to a nearly inaudible level, the better to tell him about mango masques and mayonnaise packs and he couldn't remember what else.

"The guy *you* like," Brittany answered as if he were dense. His red car doors were open, and she was sitting sideways in the driver's seat, her pale legs stretched into the sunlight.

"I guess I don't care, then, because I don't like guys. If one likes me, I'd rather *not* know."

"It's just a quiz. You might learn something."

"I hope not."

"You think you're so funny," Brittany accused in her mother's haughty tone. She tossed her blond hair, and for a moment he thought she might actually leave.

Then she looked back down at her magazine.

"Number one: 'When you pass him in the hall at school, he (A) nods, (B) says hello, or (C) looks the other way.' "

Jesse began applying a coat of paste wax to his hood. "That's the stupidest question I ever heard."

"Is not. The answer is (B) says hello."

"How do you know? Did you already look?"

"It's just obvious. If a person likes you, he ought to say hello."

"What if he's shy? Or what if he doesn't *want* you to know he likes you?" Jesse countered. "He could say hello, nod, *or* look the other way. You can't go by that."

He seemed to finally have Brittany's attention. Her brown eyes even held a trace of panic at the idea that male behavior could be so random. Returning to her magazine, she flipped quickly to the answers in the back.

"Ha!" she crowed. "It's B! I told you."

"That test was written by a girl."

"Number two," she said loudly, ignoring him. " 'Between classes, you see him hanging out by your locker. When you walk over, he says (A) he was hoping you'd show up, (B) he didn't know that was your locker, or (C) he's waiting for someone else.' "

"Maybe he *is* waiting for someone else!"

Brittany looked up, a little wearily. "You've got issues," she said. "It's A."

"What do you mean, *I* have issues?"

143

"Number three: 'In the cafeteria, he always sits (A) one table away from you, (B) with his friends, but facing in your direction, or (C) with his back to you.'"

Brittany sighed. "You're right. There *is* a problem with these questions."

"Thank you!" Vindicated, Jesse dropped his waxy sponge and prepared to buff the section of paint already turning hazy in the sunshine.

"The problem is they're assuming you go to school with the guy. If *that's* what it takes to get a boyfriend, then I'm never going to have one, because Mom has me at that stupid all-girls school. You *have* to help me convince her to let me change to CCHS for high school, Jesse."

"Why? Miguel's sister, Rosa, likes Sacred Heart."

"Then she's a mutant. Tell the truth: Would you want to go to an all-boys school?"

Jesse cocked an eyebrow. "I'm starting to see some advantages."

"Is there even one question here that doesn't have to do with school?" Brittany asked, scanning down the page. "Here's one! Number eight: 'You finally get up the nerve to call him and he (A) calls to talk to you again later the same day, (B) calls you a few days later, or (C) acts like it never happened.'"

"Hmm," Brittany mused. "I'm going to say A, but I'd settle for B. Just so long as he calls me back."

"Does it say if she *asked* him to call her back?"

Brittany gave him a disbelieving look. "I feel sorry for any girl who ever likes you. She shouldn't *have* to ask him. He ought to *want* to call."

"You got all that out of that stupid question?"

"It's just common sense!" she said, climbing out of his car.

She was wearing shorts and one of those strappy camisole things that the girls at his school were starting to break out—to much better effect. Just the day before, Melanie had worn one that had almost stopped his heart. He hadn't been the only person to notice, either. The entire cafeteria had been drooling.

"Who's putting the wind under her wings these days?" Barry had wondered aloud. "For a while there I almost forgot about Melanie, but *lately* . . ."

"She must be into someone new," Gary had speculated.

"If she isn't, she will be soon," Barry had predicted. "She can sure call me anytime."

Jesse had watched in silence, reminded of the first days of his infatuation with Melanie. She'd been full of sass then, too. It was the first thing he'd loved about her. In that moment, however, he'd suddenly realized that she'd been keeping a much lower profile lately. Why? And what did this return to her old ways mean?

*She's not moping over me, that much is obvious anyway.* Jesse rubbed the hood of his car so hard his elbow hurt.

"I mean, if a girl called you, wouldn't you call her back?" Brittany persisted, drawing him back to the present.

"I don't know," he said, barely paying attention. "Maybe. If I liked her."

"Aha!" Brittany shouted triumphantly, pointing at him with one skinny arm. "It's *not* a stupid test!" Tucking her rolled-up magazine into her waistband, she strutted off toward the house.

He turned up the stereo after she left. He spread wax over the next section of the hood. He turned up the stereo again.

But it was no use. Brittany's little quiz had totally messed with his head.

Was *that* what girls thought? That a guy only liked her if he said hello, and hung out at her locker, and spied on her in the cafeteria? Jesse never did any of those things. And as far as calling went, that was a dead giveaway. As soon as a guy started calling . . .

"Oh, no. That *is* what they think," he groaned. "Because it's *true*."

And suddenly the only thing on his mind was the fact that Melanie had called him a while back. Out of the blue. Just to talk. And he hadn't called her once since then.

"You idiot!" he shouted, throwing his buffing rag. That call had been a hint—a *blatant* hint—and he'd missed it.

*Is it too late to call her now?* he wondered, pacing around his car. *I mean, late is better than never.*

*Unless she really is into someone else, in which case late is just late.*

*Was* there someone else?

*I can always make up something about Eight Prime.* Abandoning his task, Jesse walked into the garage and picked up the phone. He dialed quickly, before he could change his mind, then shifted nervously from foot to foot while it rang on the other end.

No one answered. Jesse was just about to hang up when Mr. Andrews suddenly came on the line.

"Hello?" he said abruptly.

"Oh. Uh, hi. Is Melanie there?"

"No. Who's this?"

"Jesse Jones. Should I, um, call back later or something?"

"I don't know. She's out with someone and I don't know when she'll be back."

"Do you know who she's out with?"

"No. Do you want me to tell her you called?"

"Okay."

*She's probably just hanging out with Nicole,* Jesse reassured himself as he hung up the telephone. *Those two have been joined at the hip lately.*

Still, he felt kind of sick at the thought of the other possibilities. The male possibilities. Had he blown his chance?

*I'm not going to think about it*, he decided. *I'll just finish waxing the car, and when she calls me back, I'll find out who she was with.*

He walked back out to the driveway. *She'll probably be home within a couple of hours. She could call me anytime.*

Jesse reached for the car wax and froze, an awful new thought in his brain. *She will call me.*

*Right?*

# Thirteen

"So. Are you ready?" Peter asked Jenna. Church had just let out and they were in his car in the church parking lot.

"Yep," she said brightly, determined not to be deadweight. "Where are we going?"

"You'll see," he said mysteriously.

Peter pulled out of the parking lot and made a couple of turns, and soon she knew exactly where they were headed. He was driving to the lake.

"If you think I'm raking leaves again this weekend, you are seriously mistaken," she teased. "I still have blisters from last time. Look."

She held out her palms for him to inspect, but he barely glanced at them before returning his attention to the road. "That's nothing. You ought to see David's hands."

"Yeah. Caitlin told me. He shouldn't have tried to build a whole dock without gloves."

Peter laughed. "He won't again, that's for sure."

They both grew quiet after that, and Jenna wondered if he was thinking about Caitlin and David, as she was. David had returned to college shortly after Mary Beth had, the afternoon before, but Caitlin had been far from devastated. She'd sniffled a bit when he left, but within an hour she'd become downright cheerful, full of plans for their upcoming summer together. David would work with the Junior Explorers, and she'd continue to work with Dr. Campbell, but she was going to cut back on her dog walking so that she and David could spend their weekends together.

"People don't need me as much in the summer anyway," she'd said happily. "They can get by without me for two days."

She seemed almost a different girl now than the one Jenna had once found crying because she was too shy to get a job. Working for the vet had done wonders for her self-confidence, and running her own small business had forced her to deal with people in a way she never had before. Of course, it couldn't hurt that David, the guy Caitlin had been crushing on since fifth grade, liked her enough to come home for the whole summer.

The gravel crunched under the car's tires as Peter pulled into the deserted lake parking lot. Despite the sunny weather, there was still enough of a chill in the air to discourage picnickers. Peter parked at the trailhead to the Junior Explorers' campsite.

"Here we are," he said, jumping out. "Come and see."

"Is something different from last week?" Jenna asked as Peter led her up the trail.

"You'll see," was all he would say.

The ground had dried, and birds were singing in the trees overhead, making quite a ruckus. The dirt on either side of the trail lay deep in pine needles and decaying leaves, adding to the woodsy smell in the air. Jenna saw squirrels darting through the bushes and scampering up tree trunks. A magpie scolded from a jagged rock. And when they broke out of the trees at the end of the trail, Jenna caught her breath at the sight of the sparkling lake beside the renovated campground. Coming upon the camp that way, all fixed up and ready for kids, was almost like seeing it for the first time.

*This is how Peter must always have seen it*, she realized. *This is why he was so excited about the place.* It was no stretch of her imagination now to see it filled with Junior Explorers having the time of their lives.

"The kids are going to love this place," she told him, wishing she'd said so a lot sooner. Looking back, she hadn't been too positive about the project.

"I know," he said with an excited grin. "To tell you the truth, I can't wait to hang out here myself. Swimming, fishing . . . we're going to have a blast."

He hurried out into the wide dirt clearing, waving Jenna along behind him. The old shed looked more like a cute little cabin now, with its new roof and green paint. Throwing its door open, Peter disappeared inside. By the time Jenna reached the threshold, he was popping the cap on a bottle of sparkling apple cider.

"Happy Easter!" he shouted, laughing at her stunned expression. In the middle of the floor, a white tablecloth had been thrown over Eight Prime's trusty card table, and a fancy brunch was arranged in its center. Jenna saw fruit, pastries, finger sandwiches, and, best of all, a plate of Mrs. Altmann's homemade cookies.

"Easter was last week," she said, stepping inside.

"But we were both tied up. I wanted to do something special with you."

"I can't believe you went to all this trouble," she said, touched.

"Have some pretend champagne," Peter offered, pouring sparkling cider into a plastic champagne flute. It started bubbling toward the top, and he handed it to her just in time for the foam to run out over her fingers.

"Sip it fast," he recommended, chuckling as she danced around to avoid getting drips on her shoes.

He poured a glass for himself, then set the open bottle on the floor. "You want to eat first or take the tour?"

"The tour?" she repeated, smiling. "Is there something I haven't seen?"

"Not really," he admitted. "It's just fun to walk

152

around and see how well things turned out. You want to?"

"All right."

Setting their glasses beside the sandwiches, they walked out into the clearing again.

"It's beautiful today," Jenna said, feeling some of her trepidation fall away as if melting in the warm sunshine. She took a long, deep breath and realized how long it had been since she'd fully exhaled.

"Beautiful," Peter repeated, grinning at her.

She could feel herself blushing, but she didn't look away as he took her hand in his. Together they walked through the clearing, then down the slope to the shore and onto the new dock, which smelled of freshly cut wood.

"I think this is the best part of all," Jenna said, looking down through the cracks between boards at the water lapping the pylons.

"Really? I thought you'd vote for the Porta Potties," Peter teased.

Jenna threw back her head and laughed, feeling something inside her break free with the sound. "Maybe when they get here I'll change my mind."

"They're going to be stylish," Peter promised. "Only the finest blue plastic."

"I can hardly wait."

Wandering out to the end of the dock, she felt more relaxed than she had for ages. But when she turned and saw the expression on Peter's face, some of her former tension returned.

His eyes had gone from laughing to intense. Reaching for her hands, he caught one in each of his before she could react. Not that there was anywhere to go . . .

"Maybe if you'd just kiss me one time," he said, leaning toward her.

He looked so sweet and hopeful, and it *was* a completely romantic moment. Part of her *wanted* to kiss him. But the other part, the bigger part, was afraid. She wasn't the most experienced kisser to begin with, and now that he'd kissed Melanie . . . The thought of *that* comparison made her so nervous she could barely meet his eyes.

Still, it *would* be a way to show she cared. And if they were going to stay together, it was a hurdle she'd have to get over sooner or later.

Hesitantly, so shyly she could barely breathe, she brought her lips to his for the lightest wisp of a kiss. Peter smiled and closed his eyes. Encouraged, she kissed him again. Then again. Their hands were still clasped together; she squeezed his and felt him squeeze back. He swayed slightly, so lost in the moment he seemed to have forgotten he was standing on a dock, in danger of taking an unscheduled swim.

And suddenly Jenna realized that she was the only one who'd been thinking about Melanie. She kissed him again, thrilled when he circled their clasped hands behind her to pull her closer still. She really *was* the one he wanted to kiss! He wasn't comparing her—he *loved* her. And the love she felt for him was matched only by her relief.

"Peter?" she breathed, pulling back just far enough to look into his eyes.

"Yeah?"

"I think I'm over it now."

He grinned—her old, familiar Peter. "Over what?"


"I don't like that book," Zach announced, interrupting Miguel midway through the first page. "It's not as good as the other one."

"You have to give it a chance!"

Zach pushed irritably at his blankets, kicking his feet at the same time as if to get them off completely. His face was flushed, and beads of sweat made his forehead shiny beneath his Wildcats hat. "I'm hot."

"I know. You've got a fever, bud. Do you want some more juice?"

"No."

"Water?"

"No."

"Howard said you're supposed to drink fluids."

"Howard's not here," Zach said spitefully.

"But I am."

"You're just a volunteer. I don't have to do what you say."

Miguel rocked back in his chair, twice as hurt as surprised. "I thought you and I were friends."

"I don't want any juice," Zach repeated stubbornly. "And I don't like that book. It's for babies."

"You didn't let me read enough to find out."

"I can tell by the cover."

Miguel was at a loss. He knew Zach wasn't feeling well that day, but he'd felt lousy on other days too, and he had never behaved like such a brat. Howard had said that Zach was fighting some sort of infection, but he hadn't made it sound like a big deal.

"Well, if you don't want to read and you don't want to drink your juice, what *do* you want to do?"

"I want to get out of here," the boy said sullenly.

"You will. You just have to hang in there a little longer."

Zach coughed a few times, a wet-sounding rattle.

"Don't your stitches hurt when you do that?"

"Yes."

They faced off, Zach obviously miserable, Miguel powerless to help him.

"Do you want to play a game of chess or something?"

"No."

"Well . . ." Miguel checked his watch; his shift was almost over. He had been planning to stay late and hang out with Zach, but if Zach didn't want him around, maybe his time was better spent studying for Monday's geometry midterm. "I guess I'll be going, then."

Zach didn't say anything.

"I'm going to tell Howard you didn't drink your juice, though."

Silence.

"I'll see you tomorrow. I'm working in the afternoon."

Zach frowned and crossed his arms over his chest. For a moment, Miguel thought that would be his only answer.

"Okay," Zach said at last.

"All right, then. I'll see you tomorrow."

Miguel was at the door when a sound behind him made him stop. Zach was coughing again, but Miguel had the impression that this time it was forced, perhaps to get his attention. He turned around slowly, not sure what to expect.

"Miguel?"

"Yeah."

"I just . . . I feel really bad." There was a catch in Zach's voice, as if he might start crying. "I don't . . . maybe I'll like that book tomorrow."

Miguel had a sudden urge to go back and give the boy a hug. *If Zach's chest wasn't full of stitches, and if we weren't both guys . . .*

"Okay, I understand now," he said instead, keeping his voice light. "Maybe we'll give it another try tomorrow."

Zach smiled a little. "Tomorrow," he agreed.

* * *

157

It was almost too late to call on Sunday night when Melanie dialed her aunt Gwen, but she finally felt like talking.

*If she's asleep, at least I won't be waking up anyone else*, Melanie thought as the phone rang at her aunt's house. *Except maybe that evil cat.*

But when Gwen answered, she didn't even sound tired. "Melanie!" she said delightedly. "I was just thinking about you."

"You were?"

"I was wondering if you'd like to come up here again. Maybe next weekend? Kathy Kelly's been asking about you too," Gwen said, naming the teenage girl next door.

Melanie shook her head, forgetting that her aunt couldn't see her. "I can't. Cheerleading tryouts are this week, and I've been spending so much time practicing that I'm kind of behind in my classes."

"Maybe in a couple of weeks, then?"

"Maybe after the prom," said Melanie, not wanting to think about fitting any more into her life before then. Besides, the next time she went to Aunt Gwen's, she wanted to tell her dad where she was going—and she wasn't ready to do that yet.

"Oh, the prom!" Aunt Gwen said with a touch of nostalgia. "Who are you going with?"

"I, uh, haven't decided. There's a guy in my art class I kind of like, and maybe one or two guys on the football team. I'll see who asks me first."

Melanie thought of mentioning Jesse, then decided against it. She couldn't have dropped a more obvious hint in the cafeteria Thursday, but she hadn't heard so much as a peep from him since—not even a phone call. He obviously wasn't interested.

"I remember my prom," Aunt Gwen reminisced. "The guy I wanted to ask me didn't, so I went with someone else. He was nice, and we could have had fun. But Tristyn had at least five dates to pick from, and when she showed up she turned heads like the absolute belle of the ball. I don't want you to get the wrong idea—I wasn't usually jealous of her. But I was a senior that year, and she was only a sophomore. It just didn't seem fair."

"I'm a sophomore," Melanie reminded her aunt.

"Oh. Right." Gwen laughed. "I'm consistently amazed by how alike the two of you are."

"Maybe. But so far I haven't eloped with anyone."

There was a long, awkward silence.

"I know about Angel, too," Melanie added.

Aunt Gwen sighed. "Then you know it all. I wanted to tell you when you asked me, but your father needed to be the one. I'm glad he finally did."

*Not voluntarily.* But Melanie had no desire to go into the long chain of events that had led to her discovery of Angel.

"Are you angry?" Gwen asked. "I know it must have been a shock."

"At you? No."

159

"Or at your mother. I'm sure she would have told you when she thought you were old enough."

"I know. It's just kind of weird. I'm not sure how I feel about it."

"Well, I'm glad that at least everything's out in the open now."

"Everything?" Melanie asked, certain there was one last twist remaining. "Your parents—they weren't really out of town when I came up there, were they? They just don't want to see me."

"They're your grandparents, Melanie. Of course they want to see you. They're just . . . a little . . . apprehensive. What happened with Tristyn broke their hearts."

"It sounds to me like they broke hers."

Aunt Gwen sighed again. "It definitely went both ways. I promise you they loved her, though. They honestly thought there would be time to make up later. But . . ."

"There wasn't," Melanie finished.

"I'll regret it all my life that I didn't make more of an effort to reconnect with Tristyn. I just felt so caught in the middle, and I kept thinking time would make things right."

"Your parents should have made things right."

"I know that. And so do they. There's plenty of guilt to go around."

Melanie took a few deep breaths, trying to push down the sadness inside her. She had thought knowing the truth about her mother would make her feel better. Now she wasn't sure.

"I'll tell you what," she said. "This summer, after school lets out, maybe I can come up and stay a whole week. We'll hang out, see that swimming hole you were talking about . . ."

"I'd like that," said Aunt Gwen. "You're always welcome. Anytime."

"Okay, then. It's a plan."

It wasn't until Melanie hung up that she realized at least one good thing had come from her researching her mother's past.

*I got a pretty cool aunt out of it.*

# *Fourteen*

*I* never should have called her, Jesse thought, pushing his biology book across his desk in frustration.

All afternoon, ever since he'd come home from school, he'd been waiting for the phone to ring. Just like he'd waited for it to ring all weekend.

*She didn't even look at me today.*

He'd seen her in the cafeteria that Monday—who hadn't?—but she'd never even glanced his way. She'd walked right by him, almost close enough for him to smell her perfume. And the slow, teasing way she had walked . . .

Something in his gut twisted at the mere recollection.

*Maybe she's trying to teach me a lesson. Like, I didn't call her back soon enough, so now she's going to make me wait too. See how long I can go before I crack.*

Jesse glanced at his desk clock again.

"Not long," he said disgustedly, launching his chair backward across the floor. It rolled into his bed, stopping with a jolt. He lolled back in the tilting seat, staring at the ceiling.

*On the other hand, I never actually told her father to have her call me back. Maybe she doesn't know I want her to.*

A few short days before, that explanation might have satisfied him, but now Brittany's know-it-all voice rang in his ears. Every time he closed his eyes, he could hear her spouting that magazine nonsense about how people who like each other ought to call each other back, whether they're told to or not.

*Maybe Melanie didn't get my message.*

That would explain everything nicely and save his hurting pride, too. Unfortunately, it just didn't seem likely. Jesse could believe that Mr. Andrews might have forgotten to give Melanie the message for a couple of hours, but not for a couple of days. He was a parent, after all. Parents lived to get involved in their kids' business.

*No. She's playing with me. Letting me twist in the wind.*

Kicking away from the bed, he spun around in circles, his head hanging upside down over the chair back. *I wonder if she has any idea how well it's working.*

His eyes drifted to the phone again, his mind willing it to ring.

*This is no way for a man to go down. Not one with any self-respect.*

The guys at his lunch table had all been talking about her that day, speculation running wild as to who her lucky prom date would be. Jesse had sat silently through every stupid remark, and even when it had looked like Hank was going to take a shot at asking her right then, he'd kept his feelings to himself. In the end, though, Hank had chickened out, not willing to take such a risk with all his teammates watching.

But the next guy wouldn't chicken out. Or the one after that. Especially not if she kept up this new program of looking better every day.

"All right, fine," Jesse said, standing to pace the room. "Melanie doesn't have a date to the prom yet? I'll ask her to the prom. But if she says no, that's it. It's finished. Over once and for all."

Maybe his plan was a little drastic, but he felt better just having one. And no matter which way things went, at least they would finally be clear. From that perspective, asking Melanie out would be a relief, even if she said no.

*After all, it's better to have loved and lost than never loved at all. Right?*

"Yeah, right," Jesse snorted, falling back into his chair. "Whoever said that was an idiot."

He spun around a few more times, knowing he couldn't take another rejection, knowing he'd ask her anyway.

What choice did he have?

*I just have to find the right moment. The perfect time, the perfect words . . .*

*And then if she says no, I'm done. This time I really mean it.*

\* \* \*

*I know he's going to like* this *book,* Miguel thought excitedly as the elevator doors opened on the children's ward Monday afternoon. *How could he not?*

The book had been one of Miguel's favorites when he was about Zach's age, and he'd been thrilled to learn his mother had kept it. When Miguel's father had died and the family had been forced to move into much smaller quarters, they'd had to get rid of most of their things. But somehow the book had survived, in a dusty old box of mementos his mother had stored on her top closet shelf.

Miguel smiled down at the familiar cover illustration of cowboys and horses as he made a beeline for Zachary's room. He didn't have his uniform top on yet—he hadn't even checked in—but he couldn't resist stopping by to show Zach what he'd brought.

Turning the hall corner, he walked through the open door and stopped dead in surprise. Zach's room was empty. And not messy-blankets-on-the-bed empty, like when he was off at radiation or somewhere for a few minutes. Empty empty. Ready for a new patient.

"Where is he?" Miguel asked aloud. There was no way Zach had been discharged yet. Not when he'd been so sick the day before.

*He's got to be here somewhere,* Miguel reassured himself as he hurried to the duty desk. *They move people all the time. They move them for no reason.*

Even so, his heart was beating way too fast by the

time he reached the desk. There was something gnawing at his mind, call it a premonition . . .

"Where's Zach Dewey?" he asked the nurse up front. "Did you move him to another room?"

The woman shook her head. "He's in the ICU again. He got to where he could hardly breathe last night, and they wanted him on a ventilator. He'll probably be there a couple of days and then they'll send him back."

"But what's wrong with him?"

"Ask Howard. I think he's in the lounge."

Miguel forced himself to walk calmly to the nurses' lounge, where Howard was doing some charting, a cup of coffee close at hand.

"I, uh, I hear they moved Zach to ICU," Miguel said. Hiding his book at the back of his cubbyhole, he began pulling on his blue scrub top. "Was it that cough and fever he had yesterday?"

Howard put down his pencil. "Yes, and now his lungs are involved too. All the chemo has knocked his immune system down, and his lungs were already weakened by the surgery and radiation. He's a lot better off in the ICU."

"Okay," said Miguel, taking a deep breath. He hadn't expected this, but it was only a setback, not a disaster. Lucy Small had contracted pneumonia after her burst appendix had been removed, and she'd come through with flying colors. Miguel had eaten cake at her discharge party.

"How about spending some time with Beth Halver?" said Howard. "Have you met her yet? She loves to read."

"Car accident, right? We played some checkers last week."

"Well, she's feeling a lot better now, and she's starting to get restless. Why don't you start there?" Howard's words were a command only pretending to be a question.

"I will. But, uh, do you think I could visit Zach in intensive care first? Just to say hello. Just for a minute."

"Sorry," said Howard, shaking his head. "They don't need you in their way, and Zach couldn't talk to you anyway. He's out of it, Miguel, and he's got that tube down his throat. Give it a couple of days."

"All right," Miguel said reluctantly. "When's he coming out? Wednesday?"

"I don't know."

"What do you mean you don't—" Miguel began, but there was something about Howard's expression that stopped him in midsentence. Howard was worried. Really worried.

"This is serious, isn't it?" Miguel asked, holding his breath for the answer.

Howard started to shake his head, but halfway into the movement his eyes locked with Miguel's.

He froze, caught in his lie, then nodded. "It's serious."

\* \* \*

"What do you think of this one?" Shoving a magazine under Peter's nose, Jenna pointed at the dress on one of the models.

Peter raised an eyebrow. "You're kidding. Right?"

They were sitting at the back of the library after Tuesday classes, supposedly studying, but Jenna couldn't get her mind off the prom. Ever since Sunday, when Peter had asked her to go, she'd been living in a dreamland of formals, corsages, and slow, slow dances.

"You don't think I could wear that?" she challenged. Red, slinky, and very low-cut, the gown clung like a coat of paint.

"I . . . uh . . . Yes. I'm just surprised you want to."

Jenna laughed at the squirming her joke had caused. "Or maybe this other one," she said, ready to let him off the hook. She started to turn the page to the dress she was really considering, but Peter slapped his hand down on the magazine, holding it to the original page.

"No, I *like* the red one," he insisted, finally realizing she'd been teasing. "In fact, I think you ought to wear it."

"Be careful what you wish for," she retorted, giggling. "I just might surprise you."

"That would surprise a lot of people," a new voice behind them said dryly.

"Leah!" Jenna said excitedly. "What are you doing here?"

Leah grinned and pulled out a chair at their table. "I *was* going to study, but there's this giggly couple over here in the corner making way too much noise. What are you two doing?"

"Looking at prom dresses," Jenna said with a happy smile.

"Oh. You found a date for that?" Leah teased, but her answering smile was truly happy.

*And maybe a little relieved*, Jenna thought, reading her friend's expression. Leah was probably still somewhat worried about the way she'd betrayed Jenna's secret.

"Yep, I found a date." Jenna put her hand over Peter's. "Can you believe it?"

"I'm glad," Leah said. "It's really good to see you guys back to normal."

"Jenna? Normal?" Peter repeated with a playful sideways look.

"Very funny," she said, pushing him.

Leah slid the magazine over to look at the photo spread. "I don't like any of these," she said.

"Me either. But there's this other one . . ." Jenna flipped quickly to a dog-eared page toward the back, eager to have Leah's opinion.

"That could work," Leah said cautiously. "But I always like to try something on before I get too excited about it. If it doesn't fit right, it's out."

"Get that red one," Peter advised. "No one will notice how it fits."

"Okay. Now I know who I'm *not* taking shopping with me," Jenna told him.

"I'm just trying to be helpful!"

Jenna turned her back on him. "Do you have a dress yet?" she asked Leah.

"No. I'll probably go shopping this weekend. I wish I knew where we were going to dinner, but Miguel is being so mysterious. He doesn't want to tell me zip."

"I think that's sweet. He wants to surprise you."

"I know," Leah said, but her smile had disappeared.

"If it really bothers you, tell him," Jenna advised, having learned from her recent troubles.

But Leah shook her head. "I'm not upset about that. It's just . . . Zach's in intensive care again and—"

Jenna gasped. "What happened?"

"I thought the surgery went well!" said Peter.

"It did, but now Zach has some type of pneumonia. Miguel's really upset."

"I can imagine," said Jenna, closing her eyes. For a moment she was transported back to the first days after Sarah's accident, when she faced all the fear and uncertainty of having her youngest sister in the ICU. "I know exactly how he feels."

"But pneumonia's not that serious, is it?" Peter asked. "I mean, he's going to get well. Right?"

"Of course he is," Leah said. "I just wish he'd get out of the ICU so we could relax."

"Where is Miguel now? At the hospital?" Peter asked.

Leah nodded. "He's actually happier there. When he's away, all he does is worry."

"I know *exactly* how he feels," Jenna repeated, wishing she could help, knowing she probably couldn't. "Is there anything I can do?"

"Just keep a good thought for Zach," Leah said. "This ought to all blow over in a couple of days."

# Fifteen

"I feel like I'm going to hurl," Nicole whispered to Melanie. "Do I look all right?"

The first-round cheerleading tryouts were supposed to start any minute, and such a sense of unreality had set in that Nicole was barely sure she was there. The gym was packed with auditioners and their friends. The resulting noise and confusion should have brought home the point that this was it, this was for real, but the chaos only disoriented her more.

"You look fine," Melanie said.

"*Fine?*" Nicole wailed. Were her new green shorts not as cute as she'd thought? Was the big green-and-gold bow in her hair a bit too over-the-top? "Fine isn't good enough!"

"Take some deep breaths," Melanie advised. "Save that energy for your performance."

"That's easy for you to say. You're not even trying out."

In a surprise last-second move, Sandra had decided it was a waste of time to try out established cheerleaders in the first round. Melanie wouldn't have to cheer until the next day, when final tryouts were held.

*Oh, I hope I make it. I hope, I hope, I hope*, Nicole thought over and over. She at least had to get to the finals, or she'd be totally humiliated.

*The whole school will know I failed*, she thought, glancing faintheartedly at the growing crowd on the bleachers.

A sudden drop in the noise level indicated that Sandra had entered the gym. Auditioners hurried to double-tie their shoelaces and make final adjustments to their hair, while the people standing in the bleachers began looking for places to sit.

"I'd better go sit down," said Melanie. "Break a leg."

Nicole's stomach lurched at the thought. She fussed with her tank top, praying her bra straps weren't showing as Melanie walked over to sit with the other seven cheerleaders. A place had been reserved for them at the center of the first bleacher, like the royalty that they were.

Then Sandra's whistle blew, and Nicole found herself running to huddle up with the other hopefuls. Sixty-seven girls had stuck it out through the practice schedule. Now twenty of them were about to make it to the next level.

"I'm going to call your name, and I want you to step out and get a number," Sandra told them. "Make sure you stay in order, because I don't know all of your names."

She began calling names alphabetically. Soon she had divided the girls into seven groups of nine or ten and assigned them a tryout order. Nicole's was the first group up.

"I feel sick," a pale-looking girl whispered to no one in particular. "I *hate* being named Adams."

"Okay, listen up!" Sandra yelled, pointing to one end of the gym. "I want everyone to stand against that wall. When I call your group, come out and line up in the order I gave you. And don't just walk out, either. I want you to come out cheering; pretend this is a game. When your group is done performing, go sit in the bleachers and wait for the results."

Nicole followed the green-and-gold herd to the end of the gym, barely even aware that her feet were moving. Sandra's last set of instructions had thrown her into a total panic.

*How am I going to cheer when I run out?* she worried. She had never practiced that part. She had never even thought about it. Desperate, she tried to visualize what the real cheerleaders did. Her mind conjured up a flash of running, leaping, and pom-poms exploding in air. Some of the girls could do back handsprings, but Nicole wasn't a tumbler. Her sweaty hands tightened on her pom-poms as she realized she would have to go with those.

"All right, everyone," Sandra said, addressing the

audience through a megaphone. "Let's hear it for group one!"

People started clapping, and Nicole's group burst from the wall, almost before she realized what was happening. Shouts of "Go, Wildcats!" and "C-C-H-S *fight!*" rang from the gymnasium walls. And the next thing she knew, Nicole was running too, her pom-poms over her head and her heart in her throat.

"Go! Fight! *Win!*" she shouted wildly, too scared to be embarrassed. "Go-ooooo, Wildcats!"

Reaching her place, Nicole finished off with an improvised flurry of jumps. Maybe she didn't know what she was doing, but she wasn't going to let Sandra mark her down for a lack of enthusiasm.

"All right. 'We've Got Spirit; Come On, Let's Hear It,' " Sandra announced, naming the cheer they'd all practiced for weeks. Pom-poms dropped to the boards as everyone took their positions.

"Ready? Okay!" Sandra prompted

"We've got spirit!" Nicole screamed with the others, moving crisply through the steps of the cheer. Her voice kept the beat, yelling every word, but in her head she heard a different voice—Melanie's.

*Step out, Nicole! Snap those arms! Sharp, sharp, sharp.*

And suddenly Nicole realized something: She knew exactly what she was doing.

"If you've got spirit, we can't hear it!" she challenged the crowd with the others, but there was a hint of swagger in her step now, a touch of attitude in her smile. She was nailing it, and she knew it.

"We've got spirit! Come on, let's hear it!" she finished up, throwing in a couple more jumps for good measure. All the girls were improvising similar final flourishes in an attempt to seem the most spirited, but Nicole made sure her smile was the brightest.

And then Sandra reached for the boom box, and Nicole barely had time to grab her pom-poms and hit the opening pose before the music started and she was dancing.

*I'll never do this routine again*, she realized a few bars into the music. She had practiced it probably a hundred times, but she'd only get to perform it this once.

*Step out, Nicole!* she told herself, determined to leave everything she had behind on the gym floor. This wasn't the time to hold back or save something for later. This was her moment to shine, and she was determined to make the most of it. She knew every beat of the music, every note, every rest. Every move of her body corresponded exactly to the song. And at the end, when she did the final spin and dropped to her knees, she knew she had given the performance of her life.

*I have to make the cut now. I have to*, she thought, still glowing with her final smile as she trotted off the floor and headed for the bleachers. As she took her seat, she glanced Melanie's way, hoping to tell something from her expression. But Melanie's gaze was on the next group arriving on the floor. The girls ran out, cheering, jumping, and making as much noise as they could.

*Look how scared they are!* Nicole thought, leaning back with the relief of having her turn over. Surely her group had appeared less desperate. At least, she hoped *she* had.

She watched with a growing sense of security as the second group ran through the cheer and then the dance. She wasn't afraid to be compared to anybody up there.

"It was scary going first, but I'm glad we did," Nicole whispered to the fellow competitor who had taken the seat next to hers. "Now we get to watch everyone else without worrying about when it will be our turn."

"No, we just have to worry about who's better than we were, now that it's too late to change things," the girl returned grimly.

Nicole thought her assessment overdramatic—until the third group was called.

*Uh-oh*, she thought with a sinking feeling. *These girls are really good.*

Almost the entire squad was letter perfect, and when they had finished their dance the bleachers erupted with cheers.

"Going first bites!" Nicole exclaimed.

She sat through the fourth group and then the

fifth with growing despair. There were so many girls—and so many good ones. Even if she *had* done well, how could she expect Sandra to remember a performance that far back?

In the sixth group somebody tripped and fell; another girl forgot a whole sequence of steps. Nicole's hopes rose a little, only to be dashed by the complete perfection of the seventh and final group. *At least there are only nine girls in it*, she thought, seizing that cold comfort.

When the last girls left the floor for the bleachers, the tension really notched up. Sandra invited the current cheerleaders out to the center of the gym, where they huddled around their coach, letting her know their favorites from the notes they'd been taking. Sandra seemed to only half listen as she sorted through the stuff on her own clipboard.

"Pssst! Hey, Nicole!" someone hissed above her.

Nicole turned her head, amazed to see Courtney trying to work her way down the stands, squeezing between people instead of walking to the aisle.

"Court! What are you doing here?"

"You didn't think I'd miss it after the way you've been bending my ear all this time?" Courtney extracted her foot from between two last people and forced herself into a few inches of bench beside Nicole.

"I—I—I don't know," Nicole stammered, pretending not to see the dirty looks being directed their way.

"I saw your group," Courtney said. "You looked good."

"Good?" Nicole repeated, stunned. Courtney's good was like most people's perfect. Nicole was still trying to remember the last time she'd heard such praise, when a blast from Sandra's megaphone made her forget everything but the coach.

"Before I announce the names of the girls who'll compete in the finals tomorrow, how about a round of applause for everyone who tried out? It takes courage and dedication to get this far."

Sandra led the perfunctory clapping for the losers, while Nicole slid down in her seat, weak with her own impatience.

*Just get it over with!* she thought, tapping her fingers together for appearances' sake. If she hadn't made the cut, she didn't want anyone clapping for her. She could only assume the other girls felt the same.

"All right, then," Sandra said. "I'm going to ask the finalists to come up here as I read their names: Melanie Andrews, Tanya Jeffries, Angela Maldonado, Lou Anne Simmons . . ."

The four established cheerleaders were already on the floor. No surprises there.

"Nicole Brewster, Cherie Dobson, Darla Fuente . . ."

There were screams after every name, and some of

them were probably Nicole's. She barely knew what she was doing as she scrambled down to the floor, propelled by Courtney's hand in the middle of her back.

Sandra kept reading names, but all Nicole heard was the pounding of her own heart. She'd made it! She had made the cut! Dashing out to join the squad, she let loose a spontaneous whoop that made the rafters ring. The girls in the final cut were hugging one another, offering congratulations, and soon all twenty were on the floor.

"Let's hear it for the finalists!" Sandra urged. The crowd in the bleachers cheered.

Nicole felt as if the smile on her face could somehow envelop her whole body. Finally, for the first time in her life, she was on the right side of a cut—on the inside, looking out. She had to admit it felt good.

It felt *really* good.

"Melanie!"

She was stepping out of the gym when a guy's voice made her stop and turn back into the crowd. Everyone was starting to leave the cheerleading try-outs, and Melanie's immediate plan involved finding a ride home without asking Nicole. The girl was on cloud nine, aglow with her recent success, and there was no point in dragging her away from Courtney and her new clique of admirers, especially not when there were so many other people with cars around.

The moment Melanie spotted Steve's blond head cresting the crowd that poured out through the doors, she knew she'd found her ride.

"Hi, Steve," she said, smiling flirtatiously. She began walking toward the parking lot again, letting him follow along. "I didn't see you in the stands."

"I was way in back. I thought you were going to be cheering today."

"Nah, Sandra gave us a break. It would have been kind of redundant to run us through those routines, after we taught them to everyone else."

"But you'll be cheering tomorrow?"

Melanie flashed him another smile. "Why? Are you going to be there?"

"Well, sure. I mean, I'd like to be. If . . ."

She knew what was coming next even before he could spit it out.

"Would you want to go to the prom with me? I know you must have lots of other offers, but lately it's seemed like . . . well, maybe . . ." He shrugged, his blue eyes fixed on hers. "I'd really like to go with you."

*Good,* she thought, stopping at the edge of the parking lot. *Perfect.*

After all, she had handpicked Steve for this very reason, and she'd been flirting shamelessly ever since.

So why did she suddenly feel so conflicted? Why wasn't she jumping at his offer? It wasn't as if she were holding out for someone else, someone who would never, ever ask her . . .

"Well?" he prompted hopefully.

"Yes," she said, laughing at his obvious relief.

And all at once she realized that she was relieved too. Steve was nice, he was cute, and who knew? Maybe she'd even get to like him. The important thing was that she was moving on, putting herself out there again where Mr. Right could find her. When she and Steve showed up at the prom, heads were going to turn.

"Do you have a car here?" she asked. "I was actually on my way to catch a ride home when you found me."

"Yeah! I can drive you," he said eagerly. "I'm right over there." He rushed out onto the asphalt, then dropped back and grabbed her gym bag.

"Let me carry this for you," he offered with a shy smile.

"All right," she said, taken by surprise. She couldn't remember a guy's ever wanting to carry her things before. It seemed awfully old-fashioned.

*But old-fashioned in a good way*, she decided, watching Steve lope along at her side. *I could get used to this*.

When they reached his car and he ran to open her door first, she hardly even noticed it wasn't a red BMW.

\* \* \*

"I'll get it!" Leah shouted, pouncing on the phone. She had been expecting Miguel to call her for hours. "Hello?"

"Hi."

"I thought you were going to call me right after your shift," she scolded. "I've been waiting and waiting."

"Yeah. I just . . . went driving."

"Driving where?" she asked, feeling the beginning of a chill. There was something about Miguel's voice that wasn't normal.

"Zach's still in the ICU."

"Oh. But they never said he was going to get out today, right? They probably just—"

"He's worse, Leah."

"Worse?" she echoed weakly. "Did you see him?"

"They won't *let* me see him." Miguel's voice finally broke, and she could hear the tears he'd been trying to hide. "I'm scared, Leah. If he . . . if he dies . . ."

"He's not going to die! Is it that serious?"

"I—I don't know. I think it might be." He sounded really shaken.

"I'll come over. Are you at home?"

"Yes, but don't come. It's late, and my mom's already asleep."

"Then you come here. My parents won't mind."

He didn't answer right away. She could hear him

sniffling on the other end, trying to regain control of his voice.

"I'm all right," he said at last. "I'd rather see you at school tomorrow."

"Are you sure?"

"I'll meet you at your locker before first period."

"All right," she said reluctantly. "But remember that Zach's in good hands, and try not to panic, okay? Remember when Sarah got hit? It looked like she wasn't going to make it and she pulled through fine."

"That was different. That was an accident." His voice was unsteady again.

"Are you *sure* you don't want me to come over?"

"I just . . . I'm going to sneak into church for a while."

"I could come with you," she offered.

He hesitated. For a moment, she thought he was going to accept.

"No. You don't need to," he decided. "I'm just being crazy."

# Sixteen

Melanie hit the final pose of her original dance knowing she had aced tryouts. The crowd in the bleachers was screaming, the sure test of a successful routine. That she would be on the squad again was a given now; the only real question was whether Sandra would consider making a junior the captain.

"Thank you, Melanie," Sandra said over the gym speakers. "Next up is Nicole Brewster."

Melanie ran off the floor, smiling and waving to the crowd. Grabbing a reserved seat on the first bleacher, still breathing hard, she watched anxiously as Nicole walked out onto the floor.

*Smile!* she thought, trying to catch the girl's eye. Nicole's nervousness was palpable. She didn't look like someone about to audition an original dance; she looked as if she were going to a funeral. She shuffled out to her mark, so clearly petrified that Melanie could practically see her knees knocking. *For Pete's sake, look up!*

Sandra was starting the CD. For a moment,

Melanie actually thought Nicole would miss her opening. Then all of a sudden Nicole's head snapped up, her arms hit a razor-sharp pose, and she was off, exactly on the music.

*Geez, give me a heart attack!* Melanie thought, daring to breathe again. It would have been horrible if Nicole had bombed after all the work they'd done. She was looking fantastic now, though, giving a great performance, and if her smile was a little desperate, hopefully no one else knew her well enough to tell.

*Just hang in there*, Melanie thought, hiding crossed fingers behind her back. Nicole was more than halfway through a flawless routine.

*No, wait! What was that? Just fake it, Nicole. Fake it!*

Nicole had become confused in a turn sequence, stepping out on the wrong foot. No one but her and Melanie could have known there was a problem, and a more experienced performer would have hidden the error completely. Flustered, Nicole stutter-stepped, then did it again before she found her place.

*All right. That wasn't too awful.* But Melanie's heart was racing as she glanced around to see if anyone else had noticed.

Sandra was writing something down, which couldn't be good. Nicole was back on her game now, though, and she seemed to have the crowd behind her. She finished strong, selling her last few steps like a true professional and beaming the type of big smile that Sandra loved to see.

"Thank you, Nicole," said Sandra. "Next up is Cherie Dobson."

The audience applauded as Nicole ran off, although not as loudly as it had for Melanie. Still, it had been a solid performance and, coupled with Nicole's clean first-cut routines, Melanie hoped it would be enough.

"I was terrible," Nicole wailed the moment she hit the bench. "I can't believe I messed up that turn—I've done it a hundred times!"

"Shhh! It wasn't that bad," Melanie reassured her. "You did fine, so don't look so upset. You'll make people think you flubbed worse than you did."

"Oh. Right." Nicole managed a fairly convincing smile, in case anyone was still watching.

"Other people will make mistakes too," Melanie reminded her. "I'm telling you, you have a good chance."

"You really think so?"

Cherie's music was starting.

"Watch and see."

With songs running three to four minutes each, it was going to take a while to get through the other eighteen hopefuls. Melanie settled in to watch, evaluating each routine as though she were the one choosing the squad. As predicted, there were the occasional obvious mistakes, but Tanya turned in a performance that was absolutely smoking, making a junior squad captain seem even more unlikely. Melanie tossed her friend a few playful, arms-over-the-head bows as Tanya took a seat at the end of the row.

"She'll make the squad," Nicole said miserably, as if that somehow affected her own chances.

"Snap out of it. She was always going to be on."

Angela's dance was nearly as good as Tanya's, and there were a couple of girls after her who knew what they were doing too. Lou Anne caught the toe of her shoe on the floor and had to lunge forward to get her balance. She made it look pretty good, though, and Melanie knew that Sandra wouldn't cut her for that.

"It's going to be close," Nicole said tightly as the last girl left the floor. "It's going to be really close." Then she grew quiet again, and Melanie knew she was calculating her chances.

Melanie, Tanya, Angela, and Lou Anne were sure to make the cut; it would have taken a major disaster to keep any of them from returning to the squad. That left only four places for the other sixteen girls—a one-in-four chance. Except that a couple of girls had had obvious breaks, and at least two had suffered from uninspired choreography. That might take the odds down to one in three. Melanie still thought Nicole could make it, but her chances would have looked better with a clean performance.

Unless Sandra expanded the squad . . .

The coach returned to the microphone. "I want to congratulate everyone here on an outstanding effort. I wish we could have all twenty of you on the squad."

"I wish it more!" said Nicole under cover of the applause that followed.

"I don't think we're ready to jump from eight to twenty," Sandra continued. "But I've made a decision that might start us in that direction: Next year's squad will have ten members."

The girls on the bench erupted into cheers, leaving their seats to jump up and down.

"The final list will be posted outside the gym tomorrow morning," Sandra said over the noise. "Thank you all for coming." Waving good-bye, she walked away from the microphone.

"I think you're going to make it now!" Melanie told Nicole. "It's hard to say for sure, but—"

"Oh, I hope so! I'm not going to eat or sleep until I see the list."

Melanie had a feeling Nicole wasn't eating much anyway, judging by her hipbones. "You have a good chance," she repeated. "And even if you don't get on, you have nothing to be ashamed of."

"If I don't get on, I'll die," Nicole said flatly.

Melanie repeated her assurances, a bit more nervously, then began scanning the crowd for Steve.

She had seen him in the bleachers earlier, and now that people were leaving the gym she didn't want to lose him in the rush.

Instead of Steve, however, her eyes immediately found Jesse leaning against an arch by the drinking fountains. He was staring directly at her, and she felt the connection between them, like an invisible force pulling her his way. Without thinking, she picked up her gym bag and started walking toward him.

*Wait!* she thought, regaining her senses halfway there. *Jesse's not here for me, and I'm supposed to be with Steve.*

Altering course abruptly, she turned back into the crowd. She and Jesse weren't magnets; he was more like the flame to her moth. Every time she went near him, she wound up getting burned.

"Melanie!" a voice called out.

Steve had found her in the nick of time.

"Hi, Steve," she said, hurrying to join him. At least she didn't look so pathetic with someone else beside her.

"You were great!" he told her sincerely. "Everyone said so."

"Really?"

"I was the envy of all the guys around me when they heard I was taking you to the prom."

Melanie smiled, but something inside her tensed with misgivings. He was telling people about that already? She'd been prepared for people to see her with

Steve at the prom, but if everyone knew about them in advance there could be no backing out.

*What are you talking about, backing out? You couldn't back out now anyway. Why would you want to back out?*

*I don't,* she told herself, smiling up at Steve.

Still . . . she couldn't help wondering if Jesse would be there that night, and if so, with whom. He certainly couldn't lack for potential dates. There were probably a hundred girls who'd die to go out with him.

Turning abruptly, Melanie began walking toward the gym door, not wanting Steve to see the tears pooling in her eyes.

It was really going to kill her to see Jesse with someone else.

Miguel had barely walked into the nurses' lounge for his Thursday shift when Howard came in behind him.

"How's Zach?" Miguel asked anxiously, blurting out the question at the top of his mind. "Is he any better today?"

Howard took a deep breath and shook his head. "I'm sorry, Miguel. Zach died a couple of hours ago."

"He . . . no." The room swam around him. Howard pushed a chair behind his knees and Miguel's legs buckled, dropping him onto the seat.

Zach dead? It wasn't possible. Hadn't Dr. Wells

told him over and over that most kids survived this cancer? How could he have let Zach die?

"I know you were fond of him," Howard said gently. "We all were. It's always hard when something like this happens."

"But it *shouldn't* have happened!" Miguel could barely hear his own voice through the buzzing in his ears. "The odds were in Zach's favor!"

Howard grimaced and sat on the edge of the table. "That's the part no one wants to think about. If ninety percent of patients live, then ten percent still die. And who makes up that ten percent? People like Zach, I'm afraid."

Miguel couldn't breathe. The walls were closing in, and the temperature in the room suddenly felt like a hundred degrees. His chest heaved for air, but his head still spun as he struggled to his feet.

"Sit down," Howard urged, trying to guide Miguel back to the chair. "Take some time to recover."

There wasn't that much time in the world.

"I have to go," Miguel said, shaking free of Howard's grasp. Not thinking where he was going, barely thinking at all, he raced out of the lounge and down the hall.

"Miguel, wait," Howard called as Miguel pressed the elevator button.

Miguel dashed for the stairs instead, bolting down the two flights in record time. He didn't want to see

Howard right then. He didn't want to see anyone. He certainly didn't want to talk.

Bursting out of the stairwell into the lobby, Miguel kept running, out through the big glass doors and into the parking lot. His car was parked close by and his keys were in his pocket. He jiggled the key into the ignition, barely aware of his actions. All he could think of was getting away . . . far, far away from the place where Zach had died.

The engine roared to life and he slammed the car into gear. His tires screeched, and a moment later two rubber tracks were all Miguel had left to show for his hours at the hospital.

Zach was dead. The dream was over. And Miguel's illusions of being a doctor had been shattered beyond repair. The doctors had failed Zach. The nurses had failed him. And Miguel had failed him too. Tears streamed down his cheeks as he turned onto the road.

He felt half dead himself.

# Seventeen

*T*hey must have already posted the list, Nicole thought nervously, getting her first glimpse of the huge crowd gathered outside the gymnasium. She had intended to be the first person at school that Friday, but by the time she'd gotten dressed, then changed her outfit, then changed it again and re-done her hair and makeup, she had lost all the time she'd gained by getting up so early. At least her mother had let her drive that day.

Nicole checked her watch as she hurried toward the gym. There were still fifteen minutes before classes started.

And she did look fabulous.

*After all, this could be the first day of a whole new life. If my name's on that list, people are going to be congratulating me all day. I'll be more popular by lunchtime than I've been in my whole life.*

On the other hand, if her name wasn't on that list . . .

Nicole's stomach lurched at the thought. *It has to be.*

On the east wall of the gym was a bulletin board in a shallow glass case. That case was the focal point for the crowd that had gathered, so thick that Nicole couldn't weave through it to the front. She hovered at the back a moment, expecting people to look and move on. But it seemed the students who had beat her there had absolutely nowhere else to go.

"Melanie and Tanya are cocaptains?" she heard a girl say up front. "That's different."

*Let me see!* Nicole thought desperately.

She tried unsuccessfully to push forward, then rose onto her toes, hoping to see over people's heads. She could just catch a glimpse of a list on gold paper, a green border drawn around it. The names were a blur from that distance, though, and she couldn't even see the whole page.

A couple of people finally moved. Nicole managed to dart through a gap and wriggle to within a few feet of the case. On her toes again, she saw the heading at the top of the list, followed by Tanya's and Melanie's names, but all the heads still in front of her blocked everything farther down.

"If I could just . . . ," she said fretfully, shoving her head between two inconsiderate girls. They didn't let her through, but she gained a couple of inches.

Then, miraculously, the crowd shifted in front, and for one brief, heart-stopping moment, the entire list was laid bare. Nicole's eyes scanned down the names, hoping, hoping . . .

The crowd closed in again, just as she caught a glimpse of the sight she'd been praying for.

"Let me through!" she cried, too excited to be polite. She didn't *have* to be polite. Her name was on the list!

Pushing her way to the front, she finally saw the entire roster clearly. Tanya and Melanie were at the top, and Nicole's name was the very last. She didn't care about her ranking, though. All that mattered was that she'd made the cut!

Except . . . wait. What did it say beside her name? *First runner-up?*

Nicole felt her heart plummet. Quickly, barely able to believe her bad luck, she counted the names on the list.

Eleven.

She hadn't made the squad at all! She'd missed it by one place.

"Tough break," a smug voice beside her said. Nicole glanced over and recognized Debbie Morris, the girl whose name was under Melanie's. "Maybe next year."

But there wouldn't be a next year for Nicole—she was already a junior. Tears rose up to choke her as the hard realization sank in.

She would never be a cheerleader.

Wheeling away from the bulletin board, Nicole

pushed her way out through the crowd, desperate to get to her car before she broke down completely.

*I'll go home and tell Mom to call me in sick. I'll barricade myself in my room and never come out again.* Reaching the edge of the crowd, she started to run, tears already streaking her face.

She had tried so hard, she had come so close. . . .

It didn't even seem fair.

Leah was on her reluctant way out her front door when the telephone rang, spinning her around in her tracks.

*Maybe that's Miguel,* she thought anxiously, running to answer it in the kitchen. She had stalled so long hoping to hear from him that she was already sure to be late for school, but a tardy slip was the last thing on her mind as she grabbed the telephone.

"Hello?"

"Leah? Is that you?" a woman's voice asked. "This is Mariana del Rios."

A flood of adrenaline swept through Leah's body. Why was Miguel's mother calling her? Something had to be wrong.

"Yes, it's me," she managed to get out, her heart pounding in her ears.

"I . . . this is awkward, but . . . is Miguel over there?"

"Here? No." The question only increased her sense of impending doom.

"Have you . . . have you seen him?"

"Not since school yesterday. He was supposed to call me after work last night, but he must have come home too late."

"He never came home at all."

"What?" Leah fumbled for a bar stool, feeling her way into the seat. "Did you—is he—"

"His bed hasn't been slept in," Mrs. del Rios said in a strained voice. "I called the hospital and spoke to a nurse named Howard. He said Miguel showed up to work, but he left as soon as he heard that Zachary Dewey had died."

"Zach died?" Leah gasped.

"You didn't know that? No, how could you? I'm so sorry, Leah. I didn't break it very well. I just . . . I'm so worried about Miguel. He's never stayed out all night before."

"Do—Do you think he was in an accident?" Leah asked, almost afraid to say such an awful thing out loud.

"No, I doubt it. I would have heard by now. I think he's just hurting and angry and trying to make sense of things on his own. But it's been hours and hours . . . I really hoped he'd be with you."

"Maybe he went to school." Leah glanced at the kitchen wall clock. If he'd been waiting at her locker, she'd missed him, though. Classes had just started.

*He's not there anyway*, she realized in the same instant. *If he didn't go home, he sure didn't go to geometry*.

"I have a call in to the principal, but I'm not hopeful," Mrs. del Rios said. "Can you think of anyplace else he might have gone?"

"Did you check your church? Sometimes he likes to go there."

"By himself?"

"Sometimes."

"I'll walk over and check." Mrs. del Rios hesitated. "If you hear anything . . ."

"I'll tell him to call you, don't worry."

Leah hung up, wishing her parents hadn't already left for work. She felt awful about Zach—but she was so worried about Miguel that her grief couldn't rise to the surface. It scared her to think of him off on his own. She didn't think he'd do anything desperate, but . . .

"Oh, God. Why?" She pushed her hair back off her face, feeling tears wet her palms.

Should she go to school? Should she call her mom? Should she go look for Miguel? She didn't even know where she'd look.

"The lake," she whispered, the answer breaking over her like a wave. "If he's not at church, he has to be there."

Grabbing her backpack, she ran for the door. Her parents wouldn't be happy about her cutting school, but she hoped they'd realize she'd had no choice. Zach was gone and Miguel needed her—what else could she do?

Luckily, Mrs. Rosenthal had left her car behind for Leah that day. Hurrying down to the condominium parking garage, Leah climbed into the white hatchback, intent on getting to the lake as quickly as possible. Even in the light workday traffic, the drive seemed impossibly long, though, and the whole way there, she worried.

Would she be able to find him? Would he talk to her if she did? She remembered the way he'd withdrawn after Kurt Englbehrt's death, and she was almost afraid of what might happen. She couldn't take it if Miguel shut her out again. Not now, after all they'd been through together.

At last she arrived at the lake parking lot. Parked there, right in front, was Miguel's old car. She drove up and stopped alongside it, then jumped out and ran over the grass toward the shoreline.

She saw him almost immediately, sitting on the long, narrow rock that jutted into the lake. His back was toward her, and his knees were drawn up to his chest. The sky had filled with rain clouds, but Leah barely noticed the weather or even the mud as she hurried toward her boyfriend. Scrambling up the landbound end of the rock, she walked out its spine until the water closed around on both sides, as gray as the sky overhead.

"Miguel," she whispered, dropping to her knees behind him and wrapping her arms around his body. "I heard what happened and I'm so, so sorry."

He tensed under her grip. She tightened her arms quickly, before he could pull away.

"I wish you had called or come over or *something*," she murmured. "Why would you want to go through this alone?"

"I don't want to go through it at all," he said bitterly. "It never should have happened."

His body was rigid, his voice so tightly controlled as to be barely recognizable. Leah snuggled against the back of his neck, hiding her face in his warm, dark hair. And suddenly the tears of grief she hadn't been able to shed before rushed up and overwhelmed her. She cried them into his hair, against his skin, letting them fall unimpeded. Zach *shouldn't* have died. He was too young, too loved, too needed. It wasn't right. It wasn't fair. It didn't even make sense.

*I have to stop this*, she thought. *Miguel is more upset than I am. I ought to be comforting him.*

But she couldn't stop. And a moment later, Miguel wriggled around to face her. They clung to each other on the rock where they'd first kissed, the rest of the world held at bay by the unbroken circle of their arms.

"I knew you'd come," he whispered, his tears mingling with hers. The tension left his body as he rocked them back and forth. "I knew you'd find me."

"I would have been here sooner if I'd known. Why didn't you call me?"

He shook his head slightly, his wet cheek slipping against hers. "I couldn't. Not to . . . I couldn't say what . . ."

"All right. But we have to call your mother soon. She's really worried about you."

She felt him tense again.

"She's not mad, Miguel. She just wants to know you're okay."

"I wish I were," he said with a trace of his former bitterness. "I'll never be okay again. This is all my fault."

"What?" she said, startled. "How?"

"I should have been there. I should have done something! I . . . I should have known."

"Known what?"

He pulled away from her in his impatience. "The last time I saw Zach, he wasn't himself. I should have realized then how sick he was. I should have made someone do something *before* he got worse."

"It's not your fault, Miguel. You're not a doctor yet."

"And I don't want to be one, either! All his doctors screwed up." Miguel's brown eyes had grown dark with anger. "How could they let him die like that? Like that!"

"They didn't *let* him die. I'm sure they did everything they—"

202

"And what about God? Where was he? I thought he was watching out for Zach. I thought . . . I thought he *cared* . . ."

His voice broke on the last word, and tears spilled over his lashes again. He hid his face in his hands, his shoulders shaking with the force of his sobs.

"Maybe he does," Leah said gently, closing her arms around him again. "The doctors must have. And I know how much you do. Does it have to be someone's fault? Don't things like this just happen sometimes?"

"They shouldn't! It's wrong!" Miguel tried to twist out of her grip, but she held on, feeling the shudders racking his body pass through hers as well. Then all of a sudden his muscles went slack. He collapsed against her, defeated, crying from the depths of his broken heart. "I don't even understand why cancer exists. First my dad, then Kurt, now Zach. It's just . . . so . . . *wrong.*"

"I know," she whispered, her fingers in his hair. "I wish . . . I don't . . . I just love you so much."

His eyes came up to search her face.

"I love you, too," he said finally. "But you've got to be the last one. Love just hurts too much."

*Here goes nothing,* Jesse thought.

With one last deep breath, he knocked on the Andrewses' front door, ignoring the way his knees were wobbling.

*Just do it fast and get it over with.*

That whole week at school, he had never found the right moment to ask Melanie to the prom. There had been opportunities, sort of, if he'd wanted to stop her in the hall or pull her out of a group. But the perfect moment, the chance to talk to her completely alone, had never arrived. The closest he'd come was on Thursday, when she had started to walk in his direction after cheerleading tryouts. The only reason he'd been there in the first place was to try to drive her home, and for a minute it had seemed everything would go according to plan. Then stupid Steve Carson had called her and Melanie had turned and walked off with him instead. In his mind, Jesse could still see the smitten look on the tall towhead's face, and he didn't like it one bit. Steve wasn't that ugly—for a geek—and if Melanie had been willing to date Peter Altmann . . .

Jesse shivered. *I just don't have much time left, that's all.*

He raised his fist, but before he could knock again the door popped open and Melanie appeared before him, wearing the same skirt and sweater she'd had on at school that day. Pink socks had replaced her platform shoes, leaving him towering above her.

"Jesse!"

She looked amazed to see him, which probably wasn't a good sign. But before he could dwell on what that meant, and especially before he could lose his nerve, he plunged ahead with his request.

"I don't know how you feel about this, but I thought maybe, if there's no one else you want to go with, I thought maybe you'd go to the prom with me."

She stared at him as if stunned, as if he had just proposed marriage instead of a stupid high-school dance. Then her green eyes blinked a couple of times, and that small break in her body language gave away more than words ever could. She *was* stunned—and she was going to say no.

"Forget it. I'm an idiot. Again," he said quickly, not wanting to hear her reason. "I don't even know what made me think . . . just never mind."

Turning abruptly, he rushed down the driveway toward his car. All he wanted was to get away, to suffer his humiliation in private, but Melanie wouldn't let him go.

"Jesse, wait! Let me explain!" she said, following at his heels.

"Nothing to explain." He yanked his car door open, almost striking her with its edge. "You don't want to go with me. Fine."

"That's not true!" she said as he dropped into the driver's seat.

He hesitated, one hand on his door. "So we're going?"

"No, but—"

He slammed the door before she could say another word, letting her worry about keeping clear of his tires as he shot back out of the driveway. Reaching the street, he spun the car around and sped off, not stooping to even one glimpse in the rearview mirror.

He made it all the way to the corner before the first tear dripped off his chin. He slapped it away, furious that she had made him cry. Again.

*Why do I keep doing this? I must be mental!*

Throwing the car into high gear, he dragged a sleeve across his face.

*Well, never again, I swear it. That's the last time. The absolutely last.*

**Find out what happens next in Clearwater Crossing #15, *What Goes Around*.**

Everyone has hopes and dreams and fears . . . thoughts they keep secret from the rest of the world. . . .

*Jenna . . .*

I hope I'm a pretty good person. I try to be. But things happen, and sometimes I mess up. *You* try living with five sisters.

*Leah . . .*

Meeting Miguel is the best thing that ever happened to me. Does being so wrapped up with him mean I'm missing out on something else, though? Because I promised myself I'd never miss anything for a guy. Ever.

*Melanie . . .*

Everyone thinks that being Melanie Andrews must be so great. Well, let me tell you—it's not. Not even close.

*Nicole . . .*

Sometimes I think no guy is ever going to like me. It doesn't matter how much weight I lose, or how I wear my makeup, or even how I dress. Because I'm not good enough inside—and I think somehow they sense it.

**Coming in summer 2000!**

# What Goes Around

Nicole and Courtney have been best friends forever, but Courtney's me-first attitude has gotten out of hand. Nicole is tired of doing backflips to stay in her friend's good graces—and she's not the only one. It was only a matter of time before somebody gave Court a dose of her own medicine . . . but did it have to be on prom night?

Jesse can't believe he was foolish enough to think Melanie would want to be his date for the CCHS prom. He's wasted way too much time dreaming of holding her in his arms—hasn't she made her feelings about him brutally clear?

Melanie tried her hardest to get Nicole on the cheering squad. Maybe that's why she feels so responsible now that her friend didn't make it. First runner-up isn't good for anything. Unless somebody drops out . . .

**Coming in October 2000!**

## About the Author

Laura Peyton Roberts is the author of numerous books for young readers, including all the titles in the Clearwater Crossing series. She holds degrees in both English and geology from San Diego State University. A native Californian, Laura lives in San Diego with her husband and two dogs.